With her binding to her partners, Benny feels safe and settled. She wants to start her career in the XIA and make a place in that organization. The past rears up and has other ideas.

The binding has its own issues. Their group has to meet and greet each family they are attached to and try to gain approval for their union. A different technique is required for each species, and they have to be ready for anything.

True love might win the day, but politics is a pain in the butt.

The characters and events in this book are fictitious. Any similarity to real persons, living or dead, is coincidental and not intended by the author.



Look for me online at violagrace.com, amazon, kobo, B&N and other ebook sellers.

# Three Parts Fey
## An Obscure Magic Book 3

By

Viola Grace

# Chapter One

Benny laughed as they staggered into the dower house, leaving her parents the big house for the evening. Benny and Argyle supported Smith, who was distinctly limping from his fall while eluding a handsy gargoyle.

He kept muttering. "She tried to take off with me."

Benny was still giggling, though it wasn't helping. "You are just too adorable for words and probably the only one she felt she could subdue without calling attention to the struggle."

His black look was answer enough. The other two stayed wisely silent, but Benny could see them grinning at each other.

The party had been a riot. Everyone had enjoyed themselves, and her parents were on their way to their house for an anniversary all alone.

Dawn was staining the sky, and the dower house closed the drapes as Argyle made his way into the kitchen.

He looked at her with suspicion. "Benny, was that you?"

"Nope. It's the house. It is structured for us now, and while the arrangement may be a little odd, we should be able to make it work." They hadn't been with her when she examined the new setup that the house had made with their specific union in mind.

He looked around. "Is Jessamine here?"

"Not quite yet, though I imagine she is holed up in her resting box. What my parents are engaging in, no one needs to witness."

Smith grumbled. "Where can I put my foot up?"

"Up the stairs. When you find the bedroom, you will know it. I will make a poultice for that ankle."

Tremble helped Smith up the stairs, and Benny got to work.

Argyle seemed content to keep her company.

"I didn't know you could make a poultice without a lab."

She grinned and got her mortar and pestle. "Folks have been grinding up herbs for healing purposes since they could mash any leaf with antiseptic properties with a rock."

He smiled. "My mom did that while I was growing up. Every bruise, bump and cut got the same treatment."

"How old were you when you were given your vampirism?"

As she spoke, she flicked through the counter herbs and found the ones she needed. She plucked a few medicinal herbs and then bulked the rest of the mortar out with parsley.

"I was twenty-six. Parsley?"

"Sure. It improves just about everything." She winked and started to grind the leaves together. "I will actually use magic to make this more effective, but Smith needs to learn to be lighter on his feet, and a few minutes of pain is a good teacher."

"Shifters heal quickly." He watched her work at the process of making the equivalent of an herbal pressure pack.

"Yes, and magic heals even faster. If he was able to tap into his demon side, he wouldn't have even had to hop away from the party."

"Truly?"

She looked at him and winked. "Yup. But, as he manifests as an incubus, the rest of my night would be shot."

"I am still getting used to that idea.

We all have different aspects?"

"Of course. Your demon form is not only dictated by its attachment to you, but also to your personal magic, to what you are at the core. That is why demons are so direct, they hide nothing."

He chuckled. "I gathered as much with the public nudity in the zone. Our clothing was a bit of a jarring note."

She wrinkled her nose and kept working. "Personal touch. You are bound to me, so I dressed myself as I wished to appear, and you and the others were dressed to flatter me."

"Because you are the high king."

She shrugged and checked the mix in the mortar. "Did you ever doubt it?"

He chuckled. "Not for an instant. The first night you were guarded, but there was power behind your choices. You knew what each species would do and how they would do it. Knowledge is power, and you know a lot."

She scraped the contents of the mortar into a plastic container, and she inhaled the scents of mint and parsley. The other herbs were hidden underneath.

Before she could get distracted, she washed her tools and set them on the draining board.

"And now, we go and fix the lion."

She grinned and headed up the stairs. Argyle drew even with her and offered her his arm. She took the support and walked toward their bedroom.

As their footfalls struck, a voice called out. "Argyle, you have to see this place."

The vampire grinned and entered the room; the gauzy curtains closed automatically and the synthetic lighting came on.

Benny released him to let Argyle lead the way, and she trailed after him.

Smith was on his back with his leg propped up on pillows at the edge of her bed. The huge expanse made him look tiny, but he was craning his neck to see everything in the room.

She snorted. "Hike your trouser leg up, Smith."

He grimaced and showed her the swollen joint of his ankle. His shoe had been abandoned on the drive home. She cut his sock off and winced at the break that was visible through the purple skin and white bone pressing at it.

Benny swallowed and carefully applied the paste she had created downstairs.

He sighed and smiled. "It feels cool."

Benny finished covering him in the ground-up herb salad, and she held her hand over his ankle. The demon blood was minute, but still very much inside him. She put it to work and fixed the bones back into alignment before knitting them back into place.

"How bad is the sprain?" He levered

himself up on his elbows.

"Hold still. It was a break, not a sprain. Your tendons just held everything in place. I am fixing it, but healing spells are tricky, so I am cheating."

She concentrated and muttered the spells that shaped her focus, and her focus fixed his bone and muscle.

When the last cell clicked into place, she sat back and groaned. "I am way too tired to be doing this."

Argyle and Tremble were next to the bed, watching. Smith was flexing his foot and grinning. "It feels better and smells nice."

She snorted and crawled off the bed. "I am going to wash my hands. You go and wash your foot. I need to sleep."

Argyle asked. "May we join you?"

"That's what the bed is for."

She headed to the bathroom and scrubbed the green off her hands. She washed her face and brushed her hair, unzipping her cocktail dress as she returned to the bedroom.

"If you guys don't like the giant dorm room, I am sure that we can manage something else."

Her men were all in a state of undress. Argyle was wearing his customary shorts to bed; Smith was naked, as was Tremble.

Benny appreciated the view, but she was too tired to do anything about it. "At the foot of each bed is a globe. That globe will create a privacy screen that extends for three feet on either side. You can walk through it, but while you are inside, no visual will enter or leave, the sound is the same."

The dress slid to her feet, and she shucked off her bra and panties, kicking free of her heels a moment before she crawled into bed. She moved until she was in the centre of the expanse, and she slid under the quilt that covered it.

"Well, it has been a lovely evening and it's turning into a bright day. I am getting some rest."

Smith sighed. "Nothing else?" He put his hand on her thigh above he quilt.

She reached out and patted his hand. "Nothing else for eight hours."

Tremble chuckled and moved to lie against her left side.

Argyle was already settling in for his deep rest on the far left edge of the bed. He didn't need contact as he slept. He wouldn't wake up looking for anyone.

Smith eased her to her side and snuggled up against her back. Tremble wove his fingers around her hands and gave her a soft kiss.

"Good night, Benny."

She ducked her head so she wasn't yawning in his face, and she exhaled. "Good night, guys. When we wake up, I have a question to ask you."

Argyle said slowly, "Ask now."

She looked at Tremble and felt the slight squeeze of Smith's arms. "Fine. Would you guys be willing to wear a mark of our bonding?"

Argyle chuckled. "If you can get it to stick, I am in."

Tremble grinned. "Me, too."

Smith whispered in her ear, "Just tell me where you want it."

Benny sighed. "Good. A friend told me it would be a good idea."

Tremble smiled. "Which friend?"

Benny snuggled into the sheets and enjoyed her sensation of being surrounded. "Giltine."

Her partners were awake for a while after that, but Benny slept like a log.

Four hours later, Benny was up, Smith was on his back and Tremble was nowhere to be found. Argyle was still and silent on his corner of the bed.

She eased up and out of the collection of tumbled bedding and headed for her wardrobe. A blue cotton robe with a bright and sprightly pattern on the back was waiting for her. She slipped it on and pattered downstairs.

Tremble smiled at her over his shoulder as she entered the kitchen. "Have a seat. The fridge is fully stocked."

She paused for a moment to enjoy the view of him standing there chopping fruit wearing his shorts and his hair in a long braid. Nothing else. She sighed and rejoined the sane and smut-free world.

"Of course it is." She smirked and glanced around. Her small purse was still on the corner of the counter, and she opened it, fishing her phone out.

The message light was flashing, and when she flicked her fingers across the screen, she noted the email waiting.

The subject was *Design Approval* and the sender was Minerva. The image that opened made her laugh.

"What is it?"

"Minerva found someone to design our tattoo. It sums all of us up in the oddest way. Here. Take a look."

The base was a lion, the fangs and widow's peak were obviously a reference to Argyle, the brilliant platinum mane and the vivid rainbow eyes were all Tremble. The deer horns that the lion sported were Benny's contribution to the pattern.

"How large will it be?"

She wrinkled her nose. "It will be small. Less than one inch high and wide. If you approve this, we will have the artist here before dinner."

"What about the others?"

She grinned. "They snooze, they lose."

He raised his eyebrows in surprise and then smiled. "I like it. If they can create something that will stick to all our flesh, I will gladly wear it."

Benny looked at what he had been preparing. "Can I have some fruit salad?"

Tremble grinned and returned to his project. He served her a bowl of fruit with a dollop of thickened cream on top.

"So, Benny, what is on the agenda today?"

He sat on one of the chairs at the countertop and took one of her hands in his.

"Today, my dear Tremble, we do nothing. We relax, and if all goes well, we get our tattoos."

"Did a goddess of death really tell you to do it?"

"She said if I wanted to keep you all alive, you needed to be marked."

He paused and poured her a cup of coffee. "Then, I am pretty sure we should do it."

She answered the email with, *Looks good, ready when you are.*

A few seconds later. *Ink will be ready at 4. See you at five. Bringing Tomlin with me.*

*Great. At the dower house.*

Benny smiled. "She will be here at five with the tattoo artist."

"I look forward to it. What shall we do about placement?" Tremble raised his brows.

She patted her ribs on her left-hand side. "I want mine here. I can see it when I want to and hide it when it would be obvious."

"Would you want to hide it?"

"When I go out for karaoke? Of course."

"Why do you enjoy it so much?" He propped his head up on his fist and smiled.

"That is an awkward story."

"We are bound. Time to start leaking the secrets."

She sipped at her coffee and wondered where to start.

# Chapter Two

"**D**emon blood is a funny thing. Each manifestation requires a different sort of food to keep the demon healthy. Succubi and incubi feed on sex, warrior demons feed on battle and, of course, scholar demons like you and my grandfather, feed on knowledge." She sighed and stared into her coffee cup.

"What about high kings?" Tremble had a wary look in his eyes.

She sipped her coffee and mumbled into the cup.

"What?"

She enunciated. "Attention. We feed on attention and worship. It was one of the reasons I never considered myself to follow in my father's or great-grandmother's footsteps, they need physical contact. I don't need much attention, but I do require some to stay healthy."

Tremble's mouth was open. "You are not kidding."

"I am not. It isn't a fun thing. I had to engage in every afterschool activity that involved public performance. I was a freaking cheerleader for pities sake!"

She got up and poured another cup of coffee, resettling in her spot. "It doesn't do anything to my audience, but it gives me what I need to keep the magical batteries charged."

"And the more you perform..."

"I currently have enough of a charge going to last me for the next ten years. It is a mirror effect. The stronger the power of my audience members, the more energy I take in. Last night..."

He caught on. "You were in the pres-

ence of some of the most powerful be-
ings on the continent."

"Yup. It is why my parents always had
family parties during the months and
weeks that I wasn't at school. I would be
admired by the crowd and that would be
enough."

"So, will we have to begin habits that
feed our inner demon?"

Benny dug into her fruit salad and
laughed. "You already have them. Your
demon tailored itself to match your ex-
isting inclinations. Argyle likes to fight
though he holds back, Smith has an interest in sex that he has never let out
and you just about orgasmed when you
saw my parents' library. Now that you
have demon blood, you can read half of
the tomes that were previously off lim-
its."

He perked up. "Really?"

She snickered. "See? Just the thought
of knowledge and you want to run over

there."

Tremble blinked and rubbed the back of his neck. "Fair point."

"How long does it take you to braid your hair in the morning?" She smiled and propped her head on her fist.

"Five minutes if it is cooperating. Lately, it has been slightly recalcitrant." He grinned and flipped the braid to lie over his shoulder across his chest.

She reached out and stroked her fingers over the thick rope of silk. "How difficult of it."

He leaned in to kiss her, and they had a moment to enjoy the contact before a low and persistent buzzing broke the mood.

Tremble sighed and leaned back. "One of our phones. I will find it."

He got up and left her, so she worked on her second cup of coffee and enjoyed the noon sunlight coming through the glass.

Jessamine floated up and fanned herself. "I thought that being with your parents was unpredictable. You have half-naked men all over this place."

"Get used to it, Jess." Benny could hear Tremble talking, and she smiled at her ghostly friend. "Did you hide all night?"

"Until the moaning and laughter stopped, then I snuck over here. I have to say, I expected more of the same, but it was blissfully quiet."

Benny laughed. "We are all tuckered out after our eventful evening. Mom and Dad were delighted, and the relatives had a great time."

Tremble came back in, and he was scowling at the phone in his hand. "We have been recalled to duty as of tomorrow."

"Did they say why?"

He shook his head. "I warned the captain that we are all going to pop positive for demon blood, but he didn't care. He said we needed to get back on the roster. The team with Tearago suffered an accident last night. They showed up at a scene and a group of beta wolves decided to attack. They are all in hospital."

Benny wrinkled her nose. "Ouch. So what—" Her phone went off.

"Hello?"

"Hello, Ms. Ganger. This is Captain Matheson of the Redbird City XIA."

"Uh, hello, Captain."

"You are being put onto active duty beginning tomorrow. Your team takes to the streets at dusk, and you will be pulling overtime until just before dawn. Are you prepared to act as an Agent of the XIA?"

"Yes, Captain. Um, Captain?"

"Yes, Ms. Ganger?"

"What about the security scanner? My demon side has been a little frisky lately."

He cleared his throat, and Tremble covered his eyes as he listened, peeping in between.

"Um, right. Well, you will be issued a special dispensation, given your particular circumstances. Simply report to the officer on the scanner if you set it off."

"Yes, Captain. Thank you."

"Arrive and gear up for your first day with your team. Welcome to the XIA, Agent Ganger."

The phone call ended, and she fought to keep the blissful expression off her face.

"What did he say?"

She sashayed up to him and put her phone on the counter. "You may address me as Agent Ganger."

He put his hands on her waist and pulled her up for a kiss that got wild and ended up with her seated on the countertop, her robe open.

She wrapped her legs around his

waist and growled lightly as she rocked against him. When he reached between them to stroke her, she moaned and bit at his lip.

He joined them quickly, and she held tight as he jerked against her with a strong rhythm. Pleasure spiralled inside her until it broke, and she groaned into his mouth a moment before he shook and held himself against her.

Panting, he pressed his forehead to her shoulder. "I did not mean to do that."

She blinked. "Were you reaching for the salad spinner and slipped?"

He laughed softly and bit at her shoulder. "That wasn't what I meant and you know it. I had meant to have a quiet day without sexual tension."

"I feel nice and relaxed." She nuzzled his neck with her lips.

"You feel wonderful." He slowly straightened and slipped out of her.

She patted the backs of his thighs with the soles of her feet. "You feel good, too."

He glanced down and behind him. "And you are far more limber than I would have given you credit for."

She grinned. "Cheerleader. It wasn't a proud moment in my life, but it taught me some necessary skills."

"I can't imagine you as a cheerleader. It seems off personality."

Benny adjusted her robe and winked at him. "Says the elf who hasn't even seen the pics of me in my Mage Guides uniform."

He backed away and adjusted himself, resuming the appearance of sexy respectability. "If I were interested in that, it would be pervy."

She snorted. "Not really. I go in as a guest speaker every now and then. I have an outfit that fits."

His eyes lit with delight. "You still

have a costume?"

"It is called a uniform. And, yes, I have one. It is at the big house."

She wrinkled her nose at him, and she smiled as Smith came in.

"You two were having sex?"

Benny became aware that she was still sitting on the counter and Tremble was very close.

Smith looked hurt that he had missed it. His tousled hair stuck out at strange angles and his golden eyes were still sleepy.

She beckoned to him. "Good morning, Smith."

He covered his mouth as he yawned and stumbled toward her. "Call me Andrew."

He tumbled into her arms, and she caught him with an *oof* of air escaping. He was solid muscle, all warm and hard.

He nuzzled her neck and licked her, dragging the rough expanse of his tongue up to her earlobe.

She shivered wildly. "And good morning to you, again."

"I missed you when you weren't next to me."

Benny grabbed a handful of his hair and tugged at him until he was facing her. "You knew I was in the house, and there was nothing to worry about. We all belong to each other; I don't belong to all of you."

Tremble poured Andrew a cup of coffee. "That said, she knows you need sex more than the rest of us."

Andrew smiled slowly. "You do?"

She kept a blank expression on her face. "I do. I am just making the point that I am a person first and something to screw, second."

The lion in her grasp showed his understanding. "Of course, Benny. Sorry. I wake up after my cock does."

She stared at him for a while before

her stern look cracked. "Right. I should have noticed. Everybody now gets three asinine statements before I take them seriously, every day. Beware when the three are over though, because I bite."

Tremble chuckled. "Tell him the news."

She blinked and then realised what he meant. "Oh, right. You can address me tomorrow night as Agent Ganger. We have all been recalled to duty."

"You get to come with us and work?"

She grinned. "And draw a paycheque."

Tremble leaned against the counter next to them. "How do you support yourself? Your job as a food writer couldn't have paid much?"

She smirked. "Trust fund. Very large trust fund. It began with the introduction of vampire blood, and Beneficia put money in it the moment I was born, as I was her namesake."

Tremble nodded.

Benny sighed and ran her hands through Andrew's hair. "The funny thing is that I don't need the money. My food and lodgings are taken care of, as is my transportation. All I buy is clothing and junk food."

It was fun to stroke the mane of gold and brown into thick waves.

"Have some breakfast, Andrew. I need to grab a shower."

Tremble chuckled.

Andrew perked up. "Shower?"

She laughed. "Come on."

He didn't let her get on her feet; he held her against him and bolted for the stairs.

Tremble called out, "I am going exploring."

Held like a dolly, Benny simply hoped that Andrew didn't drop her.

It was a relief to stand in the shower and have him take her against the wall.

At least she wasn't being dangled over the stairs anymore.

Pleasure rushed in on her a moment before she heard his deep groan. She was on the edge, but she didn't have a chance to reach down to stroke her clit; his hand beat her to it.

He was careful and precise, finding the motion that made her clench around him and then repeating it. She cried out in high moans faster and faster until she gasped and her body gripped him, milking him into another spasm.

When they had finished the physical exertion and were both limp and lazy with satiation, they rinsed off and returned to the outside world.

Argyle was leaning up on one elbow. "You know, I haven't been woken from sleep by folks having sex in centuries. Benny, you have quite the set of lungs."

She blushed and shrugged. "I figured there was freedom to let go in our home."

He grinned. "I am not objecting. I am just surprised to be awake while the sun is still out."

Damp and tired, Benny kissed Smith and crawled over to Argyle, lying with her head at a right angle to him, on his belly, while she looked up toward his face.

"You are all wet, Benny."

She grinned. "Not right now. Give me a few minutes."

Laughing, he stroked her head.

Smith tweaked her toes and found his wardrobe. "I am going to go and find the gym."

Benny didn't ask how he knew about the gym; she could hear Tremble on the machines downstairs.

Argyle stroked her hair and smiled. "How are you enjoying your first lazy day with us?"

She wrinkled her nose. "It is a lot

more acrobatic than I planned on. How are you feeling?"

He grinned. "I feel like I could take a walk in the sunlight."

She snorted. "Give it a few weeks. Do you need to eat?"

His eyes grew heavy-lidded. "You are offering?"

"I am. As I told the other two, you belong to me and I belong to you. It goes around."

He grinned and his teeth were extended. She lifted a hand toward him, and he stroked the smooth skin of her wrist.

She chuckled as he licked her slowly. "This is also because we are all back on duty tomorrow night. We might not have time for a few days."

"Then, I had better make this count." He pressed his lips to her wrist and worked his way down her forearm.

When he slid his teeth into her, she

bit back a moan. Her blood leaped, and he sucked lightly at her, drinking as she slid her thighs together with the restlessness of a cricket.

One would think she had had enough, but the prickly pain and the slow throbbing suction of his mouth were really working for her. It served her right for being only partially human.

The moment he finished, she was left hot and bothered.

After he made sure her wound was closed, he shifted under her and lifted her, draping her on him, face up with her groin inches from his mouth.

She was worried about slipping away, but he held her tight as his lips closed around her clit before he lapped at her. Wet heat resumed, and she was panting as another release crept up on her. She groaned and shuddered as her body jerked in Argyle's grasp.

When he pulled his mouth away from

her, he moved her until she was curled against him, her head next to his.

"I still love the taste of you."

Benny sighed. "I am glad. You are going to be with me for a very long time."

"I certainly hope so."

She sighed and relaxed with him until the moment Tremble and Smith came back in, demanding to try out the hot tub.

A day of nothing was a lot of activity.

# Chapter Three

Getting the tattoo had the same feeling as touching a chunk of dry ice. It was so cold that it burned.

Benny's ribs throbbed from the point where she had gotten her tattoo, and she held Tremble's hand as he got his.

Argyle had gotten his without any visible reaction, Andrew had passed out, and Benny had gritted her teeth with her demon eyes flaring into life as she kept her breathing even.

The artist, Sokor Tomlin, was a gargoyle who had an appreciation of skin that was evident with every stroke of his needle. Minerva had only given him their first names, but he had gotten suspicious as they approached the Ganger property.

When he was introduced to Benny, his eyes went wide, but he kept himself professional, arranging his tools and inks on the kitchen table while Benny arranged a chair to get her at the right angle for the application.

Sokor finished the final details on Tremble's ribs, and he finally asked, "So, Minerva said you were a bonded group?"

Minerva stood nearby with a stressed look on her face that faded when Benny made eye contact.

"Yes, we are. Minny, did you get the inks set?"

Minerva nodded and fished out another vial. "Yes, the inks are primed. This is the activator."

Sokor leaned back, and Tremble exhaled while the new design was wiped and cleaned. "What activator?"

Benny released her hand from Tremble's grip, and she collected all of the gloves and gauze, putting them in a copper bowl that she set on a trivet. With a few muttered words, she washed the blood off with cool fire.

Sokor nodded and collected his tools. "Minerva, I will be in the foyer."

Minerva nodded. "I will be with you in a moment. All right, you four, line up."

Minerva arranged them in a wide circle; each of them had the liquid on their fingers that were over the mark on the next member of their group. "All right. Go ahead and put the activator on."

Benny closed her eyes at the moment of impact on her ribs and with the fingers of her right hand she touched Argyle's mark. Their group dropped to their knees as power ran through their hands and connected the circle. It wasn't fire, it wasn't pain, but it was a bonding that went deeper than the blood she had used the previous week. Their power bound and blended.

When it was over, Minerva was gone, as was Sokor. Benny knew that something was up in her friend's life, but right now, she was too exhausted to force her to answer questions she obviously didn't want to answer.

Benny pulled her fingers away from Argyle's ribs and flexed her hands. "Is everyone all right?"

Tremble glanced at her with a tired smile, paused and leaned forward. "Your eyes changed."

"What?" She looked at him in confusion. "Am I demoning out?"

"No. Fey. Your eyes are definitely fey."

Benny looked over at the live herbs on the kitchen counter. They were growing and sprouting wildly. She sucked in a deep breath and closed her eyes, willing their normal colour back into place.

She opened one eye and looked at all three of the men staring at her. "Better?"

Smith nodded. "Nice and normal. What happened?"

Benny rubbed her ribs where the small icon was now sealed into her skin. "All the power zipping around in here sifted through me, and the last energy to touch me was Tremble's."

Tremble smiled weakly. "And you have fey blood, so the eye shift was in there the whole time."

"Probably, though my relatives tend to end up on the gold and green end of the spectrum and it is usually nearly human." She trailed her fingers over the tattoo again. Her sports bra left her midriff exposed, but she couldn't stop touching it.

She looked at Argyle and blinked. "It's gone."

He shook his head and put his fingers over it. "It is still there. I can feel it."

Everyone got to their feet and started checking. While they could feel their tattoos, they could not see them.

Andrew scowled. "Why did we get the markings?"

Tremble smiled. "A friend of Benny's said that we would need them, and I am pretty sure that we will."

Argyle tilted his head. "What friend?"

Benny blinked and started walking toward the door to the deck. "My godmother. We had a conversation during my song."

That sentence got her two curious men following her and one who already knew what she was going to say.

Smith wanted to know the mechanics how she had spoken to someone while singing.

She sat in a chair on the deck and watched the rising moon. "Once upon a time, a little girl was born and her name was Benny. Now, Benny had issues and her mother knew she would need help one day, so she cast about for the best possible godmother for little Benny, and she came across something that scared her."

The guys gathered around and listened to the story.

"With spells and summoning, not to mention begging, Benny's mother managed to get the godmother to agree."

She flattened her hands on the table. "Now, this godmother was gracious and generous with her gifts. But she was fearsome and no one was comfortable around her, for who really invites death to a baby shower?"

"She did."

The vampire was the only one who was completely at ease with the situation. Tremble looked nervous and Andrew looked queasy.

"So, Argyle, why are you so relaxed with this?"

He grinned. "We live with death. It is something that is at our side day in and day out. Death is nothing to fear, only respect."

Tremble shrugged. "I already knew, but it is still enough to shake me a little. Elves have very little exposure with death."

Andrew shuddered. "Shifters have a close association with death. We don't really like it."

Benny chuckled. "I take the vampire method of thinking. It is all around us so accept and embrace it. It will not take us before our time."

Silence wrapped around them, and she ran her fingers over her tattoo once again. With it hidden under her skin, she was free to soak it as long as she wanted. "Well, as much as I love this silence, I am going to test out the hot tub."

Benny got to her feet and wandered over to the wide pool of gently churning water. She peeled off her jeans and wrestled out of her sports bra. Her panties were flicked off and set aside.

With a relaxed groan, she slid into the hot tub and settled onto one of the formed seats. It felt wonderful just to let the water suspend her for a minute. She didn't have any mermaid in her, but she still loved the water.

Bodies entered the water with her, and everyone leaned back for a nice, long soak.

Heavy sighs and low groans filled the air as they all settled. It was a nice family moment.

It was a nice family moment right up until Harcourt and Lenora wandered onto the deck and pulled chairs up so they could sit near the quartet.

Benny waved at her parents. "Hello, Mom. Hello, Dad."

Her father was looking more human

by the day. He smiled and said, "Good evening, Benny. Thank you for helping with the party last night."

"It was fun."

Lenora sighed. "What he is getting at is that we are the ones who now want to plan a party. Namely, your wedding."

Benny wanted to sink below the bubbling surface, but she had nowhere to go. "Nice timing."

Lenora grinned. "Jessamine tipped us off that you were all in one place and trapped by good manners."

Tremble cleared his throat. "When would you like the event to take place?"

Andrew nodded. "How many folk from our prides or clans can we invite?"

"Well, our side of the family tends to run around three hundred or so, so one hundred from each of you should be a suitable number?" Lenora materialized a notebook and started to make out details.

The men looked at each other and then turned accusing eyes to Benny.

"I can't rein her in. I am her daughter, not her jockey."

Her dad pitched in. "She is also an only daughter. She will have the best we can give her, and that is quite considerable."

Andrew asked, "What kind of a timeline are we looking at?"

"Well, it has to be during a full moon, protective spells have to be laid in and invitations need to be issued with all of your full names and ranks mentioned. We could wait for the blue moon, but who really wants to?"

Lenora slid the paperwork toward Andrew. "Damp or not, I need everything. And then, the rest of you." She flicked her fingers around the tub.

Tremble gave her a salute and Argyle inclined his head.

Benny smiled at her mother. "Can you

fill mine in?"

"Of course, baby."

She beamed at her partners, as they all had to fill out the paperwork with their names on it.

"Thanks, Mom."

The guys turned one by one and filled out their details.

When the paperwork was filled out, Lenora took it back and smiled. "Let me know if there is anyone in particular you wish to invite. I will offer each of your leaders ninety spaces that must include all relatives willing to travel. Nobility and anyone else comes second."

The guys all nodded.

Benny quirked her lips. "So, when do you think?"

"One month from Wednesday. We can get it all done."

Benny cleared her throat. "You will be on your own for most of it. I start work as an Agent of the XIA tomorrow night."

Her father looked worried, but he always did when he thought about her being in any dangerous situation. He didn't stop her from doing what she needed to, but he didn't encourage her to take unnecessary chances. Only the absolutely most necessary ones.

Lenora sighed. "Well, I will simply keep the meetings with the seamstress and tailors to the appropriate hours. Argyle, how are you doing with sunset?"

He shrugged. "I am even waking up early afternoons now."

She laughed and nodded. "Good. I can get the formal wear preferred by your court and work from there."

Andrew cleared his throat. "My pride simply engages with human formal wear."

"We can do better than that."

He nodded. "Excellent."

Tremble piped up. "I included my king's court and my top ten guest choices." He smiled.

Benny muttered, "Kiss ass."

He grinned. "Maybe later."

Lenora chuckled. "Benny, you have to pick the flowers and the dress."

Benny nodded. "Right. Moon silk and blue irises with pink roses."

Lenora grinned. "Good choices. I will get the family to volunteer your dowry."

The men looked at each other, and Andrew scowled. "I don't understand."

Tremble smirked. "Old tradition of families paying for the upkeep of the woman across her lifespan. The longer the lifespan, the greater the dowry."

Argyle grinned. "Vampires used to pay the dowry in human servants. I am not advocating it, but the idea was to keep strain off the mate and the local economy, not to mention the population."

Andrew snorted. "The lioness bring the territory and the alpha protects it.

There is no other exchange of properties."

Harcourt smiled. "We do things a little differently. There has been a financial calculation of every habit and projected interest that Benny could develop in the next few decades. Being a mage is an expensive proposition, and Benny is one of the best."

Benny was suddenly the focus of three pairs of eyes. "What? Do you think exotic plants and geological samples are the kind of thing to be given for birthdays? It takes quite a bit of time and money to gain a useful collection. For now, I have depended on my mother's collection as well as Minerva's, but I will have to work on my own."

Lenora smiled. "The house started her lab off with the basics, but for anything more exotic, Benny will need to buy or trade for the objects she needs."

Harcourt chuckled. "Hence the dowry."

Benny shrugged. "You knew that this wasn't going to be easy when we first bonded, guys. I am about to become a very expensive lady."

Tremble smiled. "I would never have guessed that a ride-along would have turned into a life sentence."

The gathering laughed, and Benny was content for that one moment. Everything felt right.

# Chapter Four

The next afternoon, Benny and the guys arrived at the XIA building and walked through security.

One by one, they walked through the scanners and none of them set off the demon sensors. They each picked up new identification packs at security, just in case. Benny made a face at her identification, but she smiled at the badge. It was always weird to see her full name spelled out.

She folded the identification into the leather cover and headed for the locker room with the rest of her group.

The quartermaster gave her the uniforms and her locker key. When she was changed, she would get her gear, but she wasn't being given weapons for a while.

Locker seventy-six was in the far corner of the change room. Benny stripped off her t-shirt and jeans before sliding on the matte black of the XIA t-shirt and the matching loose trousers. The belt snugged in her waist, and she put on her calf-high boots.

Benny pulled a marker from her purse and slipped it into a pocket of the jacket. As she slipped her identification into the interior pocket, she also grabbed her cash wallet. Everything else was going to be locked and sealed in the locker room. Her cuffs were snugged at the base of her back. As she latched the locker, she took the marker out and traced a small line. The itty-bitty bit of magic would keep anyone from messing with her locker.

She met the guys on the other side of the locker room, and Agent Smith whistled low.

Agent Argyle smiled. "Looking good, Agent Ganger."

"Thank you, Agent Argyle."

Agent Tremble finished wrapping his hair into a tight braid, and he flicked it behind him. "Ready when you are."

They left the room and were heading for the hall that led to the parking lot when Captain Matheson stepped in front of them. "Come with me."

Bemused, Benny led her group into a boardroom and they had a seat in the chairs across from the captain.

The captain sat down and then got up again, pacing. "How did you do it?"

They looked at each other and shrugged. Tremble asked, "What?"

"How did you dampen the traces of demon blood? We know about the demon blood, but the scanners didn't pick it up."

Benny scratched the side of her nose.

"From what I have observed, the scanners don't look for the blood; they look for what could be called a demon tie. A bond to a demon king. I no longer have that."

The captain paused. "How is that possible?"

Smith chimed in, "It wasn't easy."

Argyle snickered.

The captain ran his hands through his hair. "Damn. Well, unfortunately, it is well known that Agent Ganger has strong demon blood. The security officer was a little confused when none of you popped positive."

Benny leaned forward. "If you want to know how to design a demon detector, ask my dad. He designed the original systems, but as long as you are still looking for connections to a high king demon, you will be finding people who can be influenced by blood."

"And that is no longer the case with

you.”

“Nope. There was a spell and ritual that managed to release all of my family line from the high king’s influence. From his blood to my blood and beyond, we are now free.”

Captain Matheson pinched the bridge of his nose. “I do not want to know what was involved in that particular manoeuvre, do I?”

“Not particularly. Simply know that my father, mother and myself are no longer susceptible to demon influence, though my father and I may manifest the physical traits now and then.”

Matheson looked at her partners. “You all are okay with this?”

They looked at each other and shrugged before stating, “Yes.”

Benny didn’t smirk, though she did want to. She straightened her shoulders.

Captain Matheson inhaled, “Well, as you are our only mage-equipped team, you will have to take over the crossover calls. The seers have been going crazy, and we think another wave is building. The city is on alert."

Benny leaned forward. "Is there any idea of the location of the incoming wave?"

Matheson grimaced. "We don't know where, we don't know when, we just know it is close in all respects. It is why we needed you back so quickly. We need you on duty when and if it happens on a night shift."

Argyle nodded. "Right. Not a problem."

Benny looked at him with her brows raised. "Glad you have confidence, Argyle."

The other two laughed.

Matheson's expression turned from tense to amazed. "You are all bound together." He thudded into his chair again, obviously picking up on the mingled scents through is senses.

Benny shrugged. "My contract says we could, so we did."

Tremble chuckled. "I am sure that you will be invited to the wedding."

The captain leaned back. "So, that kind of binding."

Benny nodded. "Yes, Captain. Are we cleared for duty this evening?"

"Yes. By the way, Argyle, I am surprised to see you here so early."

Argyle got to his feet. "Benny has brought light back to my life, in several ways. My new tolerance for sunlight is one of them."

The rest of them got to their feet, and the captain remained seated. "Have a good shift."

They all nodded and filed out of the boardroom.

Smith signed out the vehicle, and they all signed out a black bag filled with replacement clothing and, for the guys, additional weaponry.

Benny had her singular weapon tucked into the top of her boot. The folds of her trousers hid the small, narrow hilt and grip.

She put her bag next to theirs in the back of the SUV, and she headed for the rear seat on the driver's side.

Smith stopped her. "Agent Ganger, you are going to be manning the computer."

She grinned and headed for the front passenger seat, buckling in. The computer was on a support, and she opened it up, searching the system for any active calls.

Smith was smiling at her.

She sighed. "Nothing yet. Drive. Head for the waterfront. It usually goes off as soon as the sun goes down."

"Yes, Agent Ganger."

He backed out of the parking spot and headed to the waterfront. When the ping came, they were almost on top of it.

"Agatha's Charm School. They have an incursion."

He hit the gas and came to a halt in front of one of the weather-beaten buildings on the waterfront.

She slipped in an earpiece and listened to the emergency call. "Two eagle shifters are looking for money and protection spells. The owner is confined in her office."

Smith and Argyle moved quickly, Benny unbuckled and kept listening to the call. The woman was panicked. The shifters had threatened to come in and abuse her if they didn't find what they sought.

She left the car and spoke to Tremble. "I am going in for the shopkeeper."

He nodded and followed her. "Stay out of the way. If they come at you, duck."

Benny nodded and slipped into the

shop, the dim light caused her to blink for a few seconds, but the scent of blood and magic pulled her onward. She heard the collision of bodies in the rear of the school, but she turned toward the office.

The soft sobbing in her ear continued and that in itself was wrong. The caller had been informed that there were XIA agents in the building, but she hadn't stopped weeping.

Tremble nodded when Benny gestured for them to be silent as they approached the office door.

The door had a chair in front of it, a theoretical blockade. The problem was that the door opened inward.

Tremble pushed past Benny, and he drew his weapon. He silently moved the chair away and prepared to enter.

When he nodded, he opened the door and rolled to one side an instant before a fireball blazed outward. Benny ducked in after the flame receded and threw herself to the floor.

She heard a startled cry, but the sobs continued in her earpiece. The blood scent led her to a bottle where a two-inch tall Miss Agatha was crouched and hiding. The glyphs on the bottle made it impervious to damage.

Benny looked to the right and saw the third member of the break-in team. A young woman had a recorder next to the phone and left it playing while she took aim at Tremble.

Benny whispered a communication spell and called for a pick-up wagon in a matter of seconds. As the woman prepared to attack, Benny whistled sharply to draw her attention. Tremble came through the door, and the woman was struck with enough glamour to knock her off her feet and have her licking her lips while crawling toward him.

Benny grabbed her cuffs and locked the woman's hands behind her back.

Tremble chuckled. "Nice work with the cuffs."

"Thanks. Getting in and out of them took practice."

The woman's body started to change shape under Benny's hands.

"Tremble, get me a length of leather from the third shelf to the left of the door."

He got up and was back in a moment with the thin leather tie.

"What good will this do?"

Benny straddled the fighting shifter. "This is a charm shop, dumbass."

She laced the leather around the woman's neck and wrapped it around her biceps, pulling them tight and whispering the constriction spell.

The attempt to shift stopped, and the young woman shrieked.

"Clear!" Argyle and Smith called out as they hauled their opponents to the door.

"Clear here." Tremble called out.

Benny got up and let Tremble take the shifter. "I will get the proprietor."

Benny walked over to the bottle in the corner of the office, and she bowed. "Your business is clear."

The woman nodded and started chanting. She went from two inches tall inside the bottle to five feet tall outside the bottle. Benny was unprepared for the hug.

"Oh, thank you. Thank you. I wasn't able to finish making the call."

"What your automated charms did was enough. I am sure your insurance can handle any damage that was caused by the break-in."

Miss Agatha leaned back. "Do I know you?"

Benny patted her on the shoulder. "I am Agent Ganger with the XIA. I came here once with the Mage Guides."

Miss Agatha nodded and straightened

her tunic. "I thought you looked familiar. Good work on that short-range will-casting. You have a knack for it."

She escorted the woman out of the shop to where the thieves were being loaded into the transport under the care of some nulls.

"What charms were they after?" Benny whispered to Agatha.

"Persuasion and affection. I don't keep many in stock, but they can be useful in their particular line of work."

Benny quickly went to the nulls and spoke to the driver. "When they are searched, look for small squares of paper or pearls or any combination thereof. They may have gotten some persuasion or affection charms in their heist."

"Understood, Agent. Have a good night."

Benny turned to her partners. Smith and Argyle were a little clawed up, but otherwise fine. Tremble gave Miss Agatha a business card and gestured for Benny to get back in the SUV.

She slid into her spot next to the computer and keyed in their completion of the dispatch order. Once they were confirmed as back on duty, the screen refreshed and the guys piled in.

"So, how did you know that the call was fake?" Smith was keeping his voice casual.

"I wasn't sure, but I have met Agatha, and she is not the type to sob uncontrollably." Benny watched the screen and she identified another position. "Sixteenth and Harcourt. A neighbourhood party has turned into a brawl. Goblin and giant."

The guys groaned, and they started to loosen up in preparation for the match.

It was quite the start to her first day.

*Chapter Five*

Giant drinking songs were not for the faint of heart, but since the fight had broken up before Smith had gotten them there, it was a good sign.

XIA relationships with the community were sometimes tense, but tonight, Benny played rock-paper-scissors with one of the goblin children. She had to play it two handed, and it was best three out of five. She lost and rubbed the goblin at the base of her skull for a few minutes.

Argyle was having an in-depth conversation with the combatants, and Smith was answering questions on what it meant to be a shifter.

Tremble was staying at a polite dis-tance from the goblins. Not all of the fey got along with them, and it was better for him not to cause an incident.

After admonishing the group to keep things to community standards, they re-turned to their vehicle.

Benny filed them as complete, and the system refreshed again.

As they pulled away from the gather-ing, she sighed. "Stop."

Smith stopped the vehicle, and Benny got out. She untied the balloon from the antenna and walked it back to the laugh-ing giants. "Here you go."

She winked and headed back to the SUV. The laughter increased in volume, and she didn't glance back.

She slid into the car again and buck-led up. "It wouldn't do to have a hot pink balloon on the antenna."

She heard giggling, but she didn't look around. "Next call is up on Gravemercy Way. We have an unlicensed rising. The mages should take it, but they are bogged down. They won't make it in time to stop it, and we need to stop it."

Smith hit the gas, and she confirmed that they were on their way.

"Gentlemen, we have a student necromancer attempting to raise her twin. The twin died in a drinking incident at the school, and it has taken Miaka this long to gain the necessary spells in order to raise him."

Argyle grunted. "I have to hang back."

"Of course. That is the one kind of magic you are sensitive to."

"I will be there if the ghoul rises. Even if she manages to put in both soul and consciousness, the degradation will have caused some rather nasty changes." He was grim. "If he rises, I will come in fast and question him later."

Smith nodded. "We are going in to..."

"We need to hold down the necromancer. Stop the power and keep her engaged until the mages can come to collect her. Just restraint. No blood. The blood of a new necromancer is one of the easier methods of controlling the undead." Benny grimaced. "But only after her first rising and before her locking in her power. If any of the dark mages know what is going on, they are going to be out for her blood."

Tremble sighed. "Why couldn't this just be simple?"

Benny grinned and put the computer away after sending the confirmation of arrival signal.

She flexed her fingers. "This is where I earn my keep."

Argyle handed her a set of cuffs. "You forgot to take yours off your last collar."

Benny sighed. "Sorry. There is so much I need to get used to."

The last flecks of sunset disappeared. Benny adjusted her eyesight and nodded to Smith and Tremble.

She left the vehicle and felt for the magic. It flared and popped all over the cemetery. A very bad sign.

Tremble asked, "What am I sensing?"

"Unfocused magic. She is all over the place. We need to call in more undead. She is going to raise the entire block if they aren't anchored."

"Right. So find her, find her fast, and you stop her before she tangles the living and the dead."

Benny nodded. "Right. Smith, can you shift and sniff her out? She will smell like girl and blood."

He nodded and his features shifted into feline, his hair wild and shaggy. His head lifted, and he led them into the darkness.

Argyle kept well back, but Benny could feel him in the shadows.

Candles flickered up ahead, and Benny eased up next to Smith. She touched his shoulder, and he waited in the darkness.

Tremble came in closer, but he left her to take point.

Dealing with unstable college girls wasn't really her forte, but she focused on the young woman who was frantically consulting a notebook as she chanted and sprinkled herbs around.

"Miaka." Benny whispered it, coming closer.

The girl nearly jolted out of her protective circle. "Who are you? I can't see you."

Benny moved into the circle of light, just on the edge of the chalk outline. "Hello, Miaka."

The girl peered at her through lank hair and blinked furiously. "I have to finish this. We will talk when Mike is with us. He always enjoyed talking to women."

"You can't raise him, Miaka. He won't

come back whole."

Miaka scowled. "How do you know about it? He will be fine. I love him and he is my twin and he will be fine."

Benny hunkered down next to the headstone, reading the name and wincing at the youth of the deceased, with the barrier in front of her toes. "He will not be fine. Why didn't you apply for resurrection when he died?"

Miaka stuck her lower lip out. "I did. I wanted him back again, even if I would live on, but the resurrection guild wouldn't do it. My grandmother is a zombie, and she wouldn't die to let Mike have his turn."

Benny closed her eyes. Only one undead was allowed per family. It kept things from getting messy when it came to inheritance.

"So, how long has he been buried?"

"A year and ninety days. Today is our birthday. I brought him a cupcake with a candle. He can blow it out when he comes back."

Benny asked, "Have you given any thought to just bringing back his ghost? If he wants to communicate, it is very easy. If you bring him back in his body, he won't be the same."

"He said...he said Mike would be fine."

"Who said?"

"The demon. A demon gave me this spell, and he said Mike would come back fine."

Benny fought her instinctive hiss. "The demon lied. Demons make puppets out of the dead; they don't give them their lives back. He wouldn't belong to you; he would be the demon's creature."

"You are lying! He said you would lie!" Miaka hissed at her with madness in her eyes.

"Did he? What if I came through your wards and took your books?"

She cackled wildly, her stained sweat-shirt and jeans exposed as she leaned back. "No human mage can get through those wards. He promised me. No mage could stop me."

Benny sighed and stepped across the demon-cast ward. "He lied."

Benny wrapped the book in a spell of confusion and the woman in a sleep spell. There was a bit of power stirring in the area, so she focused it upward and turned it into fire.

The form that solidified in the fire was a young man with a mop of dark hair and kind eyes. "Is she all right?"

"Hello, Michael. She is asleep. I can wake her if you like."

He smiled and shook his head. "No. If she needs me back, I will come as a ghost. Do you think that will help?"

Benny nodded. "I think she feels incomplete without you."

"And me without her, but I did something stupid and here I am. I never meant to split us apart, but sometimes these things just happen."

"What artifact would you like to be anchored to?"

He smiled. "My mom gave me a fountain pen when I entered college. I just wanted a business degree."

Benny looked at the objects on the ground. "Is this it?"

"That is the one. She can keep me with her always."

Benny picked it up and used the summoning magic to bind his soul to the object.

"I thought it was more complicated than that." He smiled.

"It is for most mages. I am not most mages."

She reinforced his connection and kept an anchoring and protective spell on it. No one would dislodge him from the pen until Miaka wanted him to go.

"She might cling to you for the rest of her life, Michael."

He leaned down and brushed a phantom hand over his sister's brow. "I know. I am still willing to do it. I never could be the family zombie. I had a heart transplant when I was nine. My organs were shot from the anti-rejection drugs."

Benny sighed and looked at Miaka. She glanced back, and Tremble was pounding his fists against the barrier.

Michael cocked his head. "How did you get through?"

"Oh, family secret."

She took her knife and sliced through the barrier. Tremble stumbled forward.

"The Mage Guild operatives have arrived."

She sat with Miaka as the operatives came to her and stumbled to a halt.

"This is Miaka Horrocks. She tried to raise her brother Michael. I managed to stop her, but his soul was already loosened and with us. I have anchored it to this pen. Please, please, keep the pen within twenty feet of her at all times. She is in an extremely vulnerable mental state."

The male mage looking at her nodded with a kind expression. "We will take care of her."

"Good, because I am going to check in on her. She has suffered a loss that was unexpected. She has wounds that will never heal." As an aside, Benny added, "She has also been influenced by a demon, so keep an eye out for that."

The mage carried her off with his partner. Benny waited for the next team to come in. She explained all the components and left them to take the bits apart.

Argyle was working with the team putting down the ghouls that had risen without souls.

Smith stayed near her, and he asked

slowly, "Is she out of danger?"

Benny nodded. "I used her own magic to anchor her brother's ghost, so it should be fine. There was also the touch of a demon in the area, and my magic pushed his out of the way. He won't come sniffing around her again. The Mage Guild will be watching her constantly."

Smith nodded. "So, after this...dinner?"

She laughed. "Excellent idea, love."

Tremble came up on them, and he cupped her elbow. "You did very well."

"I am glad you think so. I want to check on Miaka at the Guild holding facility before we go home."

"Of course, darling."

She grinned at him. "That is Agent Darling to you."

The undead XIA officers had finished with the ghouls, and there was a Mage Guild necromancer standing by to an-

chor those who had been disturbed.
  It was definitely time for dinner.

# Chapter Six

It wasn't a night for tacos. They pulled into a small diner parking lot and filed in to scrub their hands before settling into a booth and thumbing through the menu.

Benny was in the mood for soup and a BLT. The coffee she ordered with it was habit more than anything.

The guys ordered a wide variety of foods, and they even had a crimson smoothie for Argyle.

Tremble had to ask, "How do you know to do all that?"

Benny grinned. "You have met my parents. Do you think I didn't want to learn all they had to offer me? I had tutors from every species, was enrolled in every basic instruction that they could manage, taught by the best in their fields. I am not a true necromancer, but I am better than many trained necromancers. There are so many butterflies around our property in winter it isn't even funny."

Smith snorted.

The food was hot and filled the hole that hanging around the cemetery had generated.

The bacon on her sandwich was pleasantly crispy, and it definitely hit the spot.

"So, what do we talk about now that all the sly flirting has been put aside?" She winked.

Tremble grinned. "I suppose that we will have to engage in innuendo and seduction from now on."

"Ohh, seduce me. That would be different. Usually, I am in the mood and I just find a target." She waggled her eyebrows.

Smith put his hand on her thigh under the table and slowly moved it to her groin. He held her for a moment before his fingers began flicking randomly. That had an effect.

She focused on her sandwich, and when it was gone, she said, "I hope that the rest of the night doesn't involve mages. It feels so weird."

Tremble nodded. "You're telling me. I couldn't get through that ward and that is unusual."

"It was demon-based. We have different rules, and since you haven't had time to study yet, you won't know them. Scholar."

Argyle had healed from his scuffle with the undead. "What was I again?"

She leaned over and stroked his cheek. "You were all warrior."

Smith looked at her with a slow smile.

"Me?"

"Hello, lover."

He looked extremely pleased with that.

They paid their bill and got to their feet. They only had enough time for a dinner break. Benny got the feeling that there was more to come.

Back in the car, she found their next destination. "Back to the docks. Someone has caught a mermaid in a net, and folks are drunk and abusive. We have to rescue the damsel and get her back in the water."

Smith hit the gas, and she answered the notice with an affirmative that they were on their way.

On hour later, Benny was covered in mer-slime and wishing that she had let Smith grapple with the flailing mermaid. Benny sighed and flicked the coating off her arms.

Argyle grinned. "This is why we bring a change of clothing."

She glared at him and looked at Smith. "Can you go to that convenience store and get me a canister of bleach wipes?"

He nodded. "Back in a minute."

Smith trotted across the street, and she heard him chuckling the moment he thought he was out of earshot.

She sighed and checked to make sure her butt hadn't gotten any of the slime.

Argyle leaned next to her. "So, how are you enjoying being an active agent?"

She ran her hands up and over her breasts then flicked the mermaid slime a few feet away. Tremble was still speaking with those who had captured the bitchy mermaid because she had wrecked a local bar.

The slime creature in question was being hauled toward XIA holding as they spoke.

"It has its moments. This is one of them."

He chuckled. "You are handling it well. The first time I grappled with a mermaid, she got away."

"The lake maids have always been cranky. It must come with being unable to have sex."

Smith came back brandishing the wipes. Benny took them gratefully and started to get the worst of the coating off herself.

When she had amassed a large collection of spent wipes, she was down to being damp all over. "Pretend you didn't see this."

She summoned a ring of cleansing fire that started at her boots and flared upward with a smooth spread. Her hair fluffed out again, and she felt clean.

Smith sighed. "Why didn't you just do that? I didn't have to get the wipes."

Tremble filled him in. "Mermaid

slime can short out magic. We are also being watched by a few locals. Watching her flare into flame might have caused more problems than it solved."

Smith nodded. "Oh. I have never had to deal with one before."

Argyle chuckled. "Thanks to Benny, you didn't have to deal with one today. It would have locked you in human form for two or three days."

Benny asked, "Don't you have to take a test or something regarding other species?"

Smith shrugged. "We all specialise. Tremble knows more about stuff because he is simply so old."

Benny looked at him and smiled. "Would you have an objection to learning?"

A slow spark bloomed in his gaze. "Would you make it worth my while?"

Benny chuckled. "We will discuss it at home."

He shrugged. "Fair enough."

Argyle chortled. "That is one way to get him interested in higher education."

"It is that or hand him over to my father. Either way, he is going to learn. We have a paranormal census back home, so it will be easy to focus on species he may actually interact with."

Smith sighed. "I am not an idiot. I am just more interested in the physical effects of transformation."

She sighed. "I don't want to nag you, but we really do have an excellent library if you are interested."

"I will think about it."

It was fair enough. "Well, if everyone is ready, I will finish the reports and we can be on our way to the Mage Guild holding centre."

The SUV was loaded up, and they were on their way.

Smith grinned. "You type faster than Argyle does."

Benny nodded and kept her focus on the screen. "I used to write for a living. It rubs off after a while."

Each time they completed an incident, a blank report was generated with the time the encounter was started and ended. She had to recap all of the events including the agents who enacted the control action. Benny then had to sign each report, and it was time stamped with the filing time.

She nodded at the amount of reports she had filed. "Busy night."

Tremble patted her on the shoulder. "You did well for your first night out participating as an agent."

She smiled and kept typing up the mermaid report. "Thanks. I did try. There is just something about that poor girl being influenced by a demon that bothers me."

Argyle nodded. "Like Jennifer Langstrom."

"Yes and no. But that is what has me worried. Demon influence is insidious. It won't end just because she didn't manage the raising. He will come after her again."

Tremble asked, "How do you know that?"

"Because demons seek out the weak-willed and vulnerable who contain power that they haven't realised. Just because she is in custody doesn't mean that she will be safe from him. Her existence tempts him, and as we know, demons don't believe in self-discipline unless there is sex involved. Even then, it is easier with a partner to do the disciplining."

Smith scowled. "You think she has been sexually interfered with?"

Benny shook her head. "Nothing like that. She was given hope, and now that it has been removed, she will be looking to replace that vacancy of need and want that drove her forward. She will be more vulnerable than before."

Smith asked, "Can her brother's ghost be turned?"

She sighed. "No. That I can be confident of. Demon magic repels demon magic. If anyone tries to hack through that spell, I will feel it."

"Can they trace it back to you?"

She snorted and completed the arrest report on the mermaid.

"Yes. He can definitely trace the spell back to me, but he won't. As strong as his spells were, I could pass through them without trouble. He is a manipulator and I am way past being susceptible to that kind of bullshit." She watched the streets flow past.

Argyle broke the silence. "Were you susceptible once?"

She nodded. "I kept the silence for a while, but eventually, I told my parents. It was the last demon incident recorded in Redbird City before my parents' abduction."

"What did he offer you?"

"Normality. He said he could take my power and leave me a nice, normal, teenage girl. My father had changed, and my mother...well, she was still my mother, but it was different. Her illness had changed us all. Since they were sharing a soul, I felt lost, out of the loop. He said he could change it, make it like it was before. It was my lowest moment and I agreed, but not before I told my dad."

Tremble reached forward again and squeezed her shoulder.

"Harcourt intervened, and I found the motives of Jimhal the demon as they were brought into the open."

Smith asked, "Could this be Jimhal?"

Benny closed her eyes and remembered the blood and dismemberment. "No. Jimhal will never appear on this plane again. He is extremely dead. Dad offered him a chance to give up the prize he was seeking. Jimhal wanted to fight Dad for the territory of my mind and body; he lost." Benny chuckled weakly. "I don't think he ever realised that he was facing my father. If he did, he realised it too late."

Smith hissed. "That would be a mistake. Harcourt looks like he can take a hit."

"You have no idea."

She glanced back at Argyle, and he was opening and closing his fists.

"We are here."

Her attention was brought around to the building in front of them. "I don't know how long I will be. If I am too late, head for the agency and send Pooky to bring me home."

"We will wait for you. We are a team, Benny. We won't leave you behind."

She flashed a smile and left the car, covering herself in human-based magic.

She showed her credentials to the desk sergeant. "I am here to see a woman arrested earlier this evening. Miaka Horrocks."

He flicked through his records and nodded. "She is in holding."

"I need to speak with her. I am concerned for her wellbeing."

He blinked. "We know how to treat our own here."

"She may well be a target for a demon, and I am better equipped to deal with that than you are."

"Why is that?" His smug look told her that he wasn't going to let her in.

"I was raised by one." She let her eyes flare demon green, and then, she flicked them into brilliant fey colours.

By the time his startled shout brought backup, she looked like a half-elf.

It was easy to get his superior to let her in. The desk sergeant was obviously in need of a break if he couldn't tell the difference between fey eyes and demon eyes.

She was escorted in to the holding area, and she sought the pen. "Excuse me. She was brought in with a pen."

"It has been logged into evidence."

"Unlog it. It has her brother's soul in it, and he will be able to keep her calm. Consider him a second witness."

"She didn't mention it."

Benny sighed. "She didn't know, but I explained things in detail to the transporting officers. I am guessing that they just got busy and didn't mean to drive her mad. Please bring it and put it outside the cell."

Benny was let into Miaka's cell, and the woman was rocking violently, pulling on her hair.

"Oh, Miaka. What are you doing?"

"He's gone; he's gone. He's lost and it is all my fault."

Benny touched Miaka's cheek to get

the young woman to look at her. "He isn't gone. He is nearby. Wait just a moment."

Benny waited until the officer opened the door for her, and she smiled politely. "Where is the pen?"

"There is no record of it."

"Do you mind if I find it?"

The officer smirked. "Go for it. The officers who brought her in are back on the street."

Benny held out her hand and summoned the pen, and just to be nasty, she pulled the uniform of the officer who had it on him. Dark fabric landed in her palm, and with a little investigation, she found the pen.

The officer across from her was staring. "You took their uniform?"

"Oh, you know XIA magic. It is messy."

"Can you put the clothing back?"

Benny sighed. "I am afraid not. I

don't know who it came from. I just tracked the pen and pulled everything around it to keep it safe. I didn't want it to snag on anything."

She looked at the pen and whispered, "Michael, she needs you."

The ghost appeared and walked through the door to his sister.

The sobbing turned from panicked to delighted. Miaka was coming back to herself and swirling into her new reality.

The conversation between the twins began, and Benny looked around for a safe place to put the pen.

The officer was digging through the clothing and found the identity badge. The call was immediately placed and the nearly naked officer located.

When the officer questioned why the pen had been on his person, Benny could clearly hear him say that he wasn't going to take orders from an XIA agent.

Benny raised her eyebrows at the officer on this side of the call. Colour crept into his face.

Benny used a small charm to stick the pen to the wall next to the cell.

"I will be checking in with her later, and I will file paperwork to get her transferred to the XIA. We actually do know how to handle our own, and we have compassion for those who end up in a place that their genetic inheritance put them in."

She checked on Miaka again, and the woman was eagerly speaking to her brother.

Michael glanced at Benny and inclined his head. She nodded back and left them to their reunion.

A small enchantment to tie Miaka to the pen was the same one that Lenora used to use so that Benny didn't lose her homework.

Benny inclined her head to the officer walking her around, and she left the building. One more batch of paperwork was in her future, and the sooner she got to the SUV, the better.

# Chapter Seven

The guys saw her coming and straightened from their positions loitering on the SUV. Tremble summed it up. "Uh, oh."

Benny got into the seat and fired up the computer, writing a scathing report and request for prisoner transfer. When it came to the reasoning, she smirked and wrote that as the XIA agents had had to fend off the ghouls, it was their jurisdiction that had been impinged.

The rest of the prisoner torture was recorded, including the name of Mage Guild Officer Ambrican, who had removed the pen and kept it for his own purposes.

She outlined her summoning of the pen and the uniform that came with it, culminating with her attaching the pen to the prisoner via spell work, while the others climbed into the vehicle.

"What happened in there?" Argyle asked cautiously.

Smith pulled away from the parking spot and headed around the block to the XIA.

"They had her in an isolated cell and didn't put the pen close enough for activation. She was going insane at an accelerated rate, and the break in her spell only made it worse."

Tremble's voice was soft. "So, you are angry."

"Furious. I would have taken her out of there if she hadn't been on record with all agencies." Benny kept typing until she had assembled a complete assessment of the situation and her actions. When she sent the file, she closed the computer and her hands formed fists in her lap.

Cautiously, Argyle asked, "Why are you so angered by this?"

Benny worked at calming herself. Her eyes were flicking between glowing demon green and rainbow fey with rapid cycling. She could feel it.

The new change to her social structure was a source of stress. She hadn't found a normal balance and now something was hitting one of her hot buttons. Too much too soon.

Tremble put his hand on her shoulder again, and she breathed slowly, using his aura to calm herself. Between him and Argyle, she could probably anchor her mood to theirs and keep herself stable, but if either of them pitched a mood, she would go along for the ride. It was better to figure out a way to calm herself.

When they returned to the agency, she headed inside with her team and changed back into her normal clothing. Her locker hadn't been tampered with while she was gone, and it was one relief in a messed-up evening.

"Ganger. In my office."

The captain's voice rapped out. She turned and headed to the sound of the irritated commanding officer.

"Close the door."

She stood in front of the captain's desk. "Yes, Captain."

He looked at her and cocked his head. "Why did you do that? The Horrocks woman was off our books."

"She was going insane. In a matter of hours, she would have been catatonic, and from there, she would have been prime psychic fodder for the demon who was sponsoring her."

Matheson leaned back in his chair. "How do you know that?"

"I was once the target of a similar pattern of attack. Demons go with what works."

"How was it resolved in your case?"

She stared straight ahead. "My father intervened."

"And you intervened in the case of Miss Horrocks. Well, since you have legitimate reason to believe that a demon is involved and the Mage Guild does not want to draw the attention of one unless necessary, we are taking possession of the woman and her brother."

Benny nearly collapsed with relief. "I can help with warding a safe spot for her. She will need help developing mental skills and defenses to keep him out."

Captain Matheson held up a hand. "We call in specialists for that sort of thing, but it has been so long since there was a demon on the books that I will have to dig out the contact information."

"She will get help?"

"You can come in early and check on her tomorrow. For tonight, just put a ward around the room we are putting her in. Is that acceptable?"

Benny nodded. "Yes, Captain. Thank you."

Matheson sighed and ran a hand through his hair. "You were very careful to not incriminate your partners."

"I was doing my part as the mage-humanish part of the grouping."

"Well, you filled a position that we didn't even know was lacking."

"Argyle and Tremble managed to keep the ghouls confined. Smith located the mage and watched my back."

"So, a well-rounded team. Good work for your first night; now, come on and ward that cell."

Benny followed him, and her team followed her. They went down to the cells, and Benny eyed the sparse room with a wrinkled nose.

"Can I make it more comfortable?"

Matheson raised his brows. "Can

you?"

She stepped in and thickened the pad of the bed with a whispered enchantment. The floor was sealed with a glyph that she drew with her shoe. It was warmed to a comfortable temperature, and when she had made it as physically comfortable as she could, she walked up to Argyle. "Bite my thumb, please."

He blinked, but obliged.

She hissed as her skin was punctured and cupped her hand so as not to waste the blood.

"Smith, can you give me a boost?"

He came in after her and offered his cupped hands. She awkwardly got up and hands cupped her backside to steady her. "Thanks, Tremble."

Wards could be made of anything, but if you were trying to keep out a demon, it had to be blood. She pressed a dot to the corner and jerked her head to the right. They carried her to the next corner, and she marked it as well. When all four were treated, they set her down and she went to where the wall met the floor and repeated the anointing. She washed her thumb and was about to stick it in her mouth when Argyle grabbed her hand and sucked it like a lollipop.

She knew the moment the puncture sealed. He withdrew her finger and gave her a tiny kiss and a wink.

"Wait out there." Benny faced the room and sent magic out to cast a web across the walls, floor and ceiling. No demon but Benny could cross the boundary, and no hostile intent could pass through the door.

She was a little dizzy when she was done, but it was a solid piece of enchantment.

Captain Matheson looked at her and nodded. "Smith, you had better get her home. She looks exhausted."

"Yes, Captain."

They were on their way out when Miaka and her spectral brother were on the way in. When Miaka saw her, the woman broke free and collided bodily with Benny. Her cuffs were still in place, but she whispered, "Thank you."

Benny teared up, and she pressed her head to Miaka's. "You will be safe here. I will talk with you when I come back on shift."

"Michael can stay with me?"

"He can. He can be with you as long as you need him."

The agent behind Miaka nodded and patted his pocket where the pen resided. "It will remain in an active distance."

Benny smiled. "Thanks."

She didn't mention that the pen would move on its own now, that wasn't something she wanted to announced considering that she had just gotten the very unstable girl into a place that respected the trauma that had created the illegal activity. She would get a fair run at justice.

Benny backed off, and Miaka was taken down the hall to her room. She should be comfortable enough until the following day.

Benny was in dire need of a nap. She had used a lot of magic, and since it was coming from her alone, it was taking its toll.

Her crew was waiting for her, and they all stumbled out into the pinking dawn. Pooky was waiting, and he shepherded them home in no time. They all needed to rest, and it was no surprise that they all chose her bed to climb into. The discomfort of a jumble of limbs took second place to the need to sleep.

Benny woke with a jolt that sent Tremble and Andrew into high alert. Argyle leaned up on an elbow and raised his eyebrows. "What is it, Benny? Something wrong?"

The other two were looking around as if preparing for an incursion, but Argyle had it right. Something was pulling her.

She got up and put on a robe, heading downstairs to check her phone. "I will be back in a minute."

The impulse that pulled her downstairs was a new one.

Her phone was hovering above the counter where she had left it, and all the lights it had available were flashing.

When Benny reached the phone, it quieted and settled against her palm.

Two lines of text from an unexpected source was displayed on the screen.

*I need to speak with you about the pending case. Meet me at the Wicked Brew; I will be there all day.*

Benny blinked. "Right. I need a shower."

The origin of the text was unknown to her phone, but the feel of the power was eerily familiar. Jennifer Langstrom had the unusual distinction of having a mind and aura patterned like Benny's, without the power. Benny had attempted to strip the soul copy off of Jennifer, but the layer underneath had taken to the imprint.

One short phone call had been all they had been allowed before her lawyers had told her to stop talking to Benny. If she wanted to meet in person, it had to be important. During her training, the XIA had recommended that Benny not meet her, but something was up.

She trotted upstairs and headed into the shower, locking out any of her companions. She didn't want company and definitely no shenanigans before she left.

Wrapped in a towel, she returned to the bedroom and filled in her collection.

"I got a text from a friend. I have to meet her for coffee."

Tremble stood and headed for the shower. "I am coming with you."

She twisted her head toward him and followed him into the bathroom. "Why?"

"That was way too much power for a simple request." He smirked and pushed her out of the bathroom, closing and locking the door.

Sighing, she headed for her wardrobe, and she pulled out her normal collection of jeans, t-shirt and underwear. When she was dry and dressed, she pulled a brush through her hair in time to see Tremble emerge from the bathroom with his hair braided for the day.

She walked to the side of the bed where Andrew was watching her, and she rubbed her cheek against his. "See you in a few hours."

He blinked and rubbed his eyes. "What time is it?"

Argyle snorted. "It is ten in the morning."

Benny winced. "Sorry. If it wasn't a friend, I wouldn't go, but she needs to talk and we can't discuss things over the phone."

Andrew sighed. "Talk to you later."

He dropped back into the pillows, and she laughed.

Argyle beckoned to her, and she walked around the bed to cuddle with him for a moment before Tremble cleared his throat.

"Ready."

Argyle leaned back and slept instantly with a slight smile on his face.

There was only time for a glass of water before she hauled Tremble out and into the sunlight. Pooky galloped around and became his normal sports-car configuration.

"Sorry for the sudden need, Pooky. I got a call." She settled her small purse between the front seats.

Tremble slid and glanced at her. "Are you going to tell me where we are going and who we are meeting?"

Pooky started to roll down the driveway.

"We are going to Wicked Brew, and I am going to have a conversation with Jennifer Langstrom. She has information about the pending lawsuit."

He blinked. "What lawsuit?"

"Oh. Damn. I forgot this hit the fan when I was in training and you guys were on leave. Um...My parents are being sued for the wilful neglect that led to the death of the other girls and the endangerment of Jennifer."

Tremble cleared his throat. "You did forget to mention that."

"Sorry. I got distracted with the demon thing and all."

He sighed and closed his eyes. "Why are you going to meet with her today? I would think her lawyer would have told her to stay away."

Benny shrugged. "I have no idea. That is what we are going to find out."

Tremble sighed. "This is a bad idea."

She chuckled and squeezed his hand. "Like many others I have had, I am sure things will turn out fine...eventually."

He gave her a wry look through his rainbow eyes. "Don't think that wearing fey eyes will make me soften on this. It is not a good idea."

She let Pooky drive, he was doing it anyway, and looked at her face in the driver's mirror for an instant. "I didn't mean to. I am guessing that things are shifting. Let's wait and see how they work out."

# Chapter Eight

Jennifer was sitting with a cup between her palms in a quiet corner of the busiest coffee shop in town.

Benny placed her order and moved to sit across from Jennifer. "You rang?"

Jennifer's eyes were hollow and haunted. She reached out and touched Benny's hand, sighing in relief. "I have missed that."

Benny's eyes teared up. "I am sorry, but I had to pull the copy off you."

Jennifer nodded and swallowed. "I understand. I didn't want to file charges, but my parents took over."

"It is fine. We will get through it, I am sure."

Jennifer nodded, and the foam on her cappuccino began to stir.

"I needed to speak with you in order to give you a warning or instruction. I am not sure."

Benny looked into the face of what had obviously become a seer. "I am listening."

Jennifer squeezed her hand. "See the fey first. Call the wild and see the fey first. Wear all that you have when you see them. It is important. All of you must wear all that you are."

The cryptic nature of the reading didn't bug Benny. She had been seered before.

Jennifer blinked and sighed, looking into her cup warily. "You know, I used to drink my coffee black, but now, I see too much in it. Is it the template?"

"No. It is the print of magic laid on your mind. You are now pulling wild magic into you, and it is coming in the form of time. Every seer is born to pull one wavelength."

"How do you know mine is time?"

"It feels like time."

Jennifer rubbed her forehead. "Why won't it shut off?"

Benny grabbed a napkin with her free hand and started writing with a pen groped from her purse. "Call this guy and tell him two things. One, I sent you, and two, you are a time seer. He will help train you. Your mind no longer has the automatic structure to process power. You are going to have to go into training or go insane."

Jennifer took the napkin with a shaking hand. "It's a man?"

Benny grinned. "He is the best trainer for you. Female seers grow into their powers. He acquired his, and he can help you start from the basics. He has gone through it himself."

Jennifer nodded and seemed content

to ignore the lack of direct answer. "Right. One more thing. What is his name?"

Benny chuckled. "I am not authorised to use it. He is a name seer. That is how he looks forward and back. You use time and follow the magic, he uses names and sees where they go and where they have been, forward and backward in time. I think you two will get along."

"Thank you. I know things are about to hit the fan. Thank you for coming when I called."

Benny smiled. "It is the least I can do for what was done to you, but you saved my life."

Jennifer smiled. "You saved mine. I am just beginning to know my own mind, so when I know how I feel about the whole thing, I will let you know."

"Be sure you do. If you want to attack, I am ready for it."

Benny got to her feet and took her

mochachino from the server and gripped the takeaway cup. "Thank you."

The server nodded and smiled.

She turned back to Jennifer. "Take care and call if you need anything."

Jennifer smiled and held up the napkin. "This feels like what I needed."

They parted ways without saying goodbye.

Benny beckoned to Tremble, and he pried himself away from the ladies sighing over him.

Tremble murmured outside, "She doesn't look good."

"No, she is going mad."

Benny didn't look back, but she could feel Jennifer's gaze on them as they got into Pooky and she gave the order to go to the XIA so she could check on Miaka.

Tremble and Benny passed through security and got authorisation to visit Miaka. He went to check their schedule while she headed to holding.

Miaka was with Michael in an interview room, and a necromancer was interviewing her.

Benny tapped on the door, and Miaka smiled, asking quickly if Benny could enter. The bemused necromancer nodded.

Benny entered and moved to put her hand on Miaka's shoulder. "How are you feeling?"

"Much better. Officer Demorak was just having me walk through the rituals of last night. I had to confess that you were the one who handled Michael."

Michael grinned. "I was hardly handled."

"Agent Ganger, perhaps you could tell me what spell you used?"

Benny nodded to Officer Demorak and smiled. "Miaka raised her twin, and I anchored him to the pen using an association connection. As long as he wants to manifest, he will be bound to that pen."

The officer blinked. "You gave the ghost the choice?"

"Of course. It is his afterlife he is delaying. When he and Miaka decide she no longer needs him with her every day, they will discuss it and he can be released, by his own will or hers."

"How did you manage that?"

Benny snorted at the obvious answer. "They are twins. Joined in blood and soul."

The officer struck his forehead with his palm. "Right. Not necromancy, binding magic."

Benny winked at Miaka. "I have a knack for muddling magics."

Miaka smiled. "I am glad for it."

"Well, you seem to be doing fine. I just wanted to check on you."

Miaka sighed. "Thank you. You kept your word."

Benny winked again. "Now, I have to get the elf back to bed. He is getting all grouchy."

Officer Demorak stared. "You are the agents who dealt with that demon issue."

Benny grinned. "We are. Now, I will be leaving. I will be back this evening and check on you again before dawn, Miaka, Michael."

Michael smiled and put his hand on his sister's shoulder. It was a spectral effort, but Miaka relaxed at the phantom contact. "We look forward to the visit."

Benny left, and when she was outside the room, the door opened and closed behind her. Officer Demorak grabbed her arm. "How did you do it?"

"What?"

"How did you anchor him like that?"

Tremble was moving toward them with a scowl on his elegant features. His gaze was fixed on the hand on her arm.

"If you have to know, it was demon magic. Soul manipulation to achieve a purpose. There was a touch of vampire reanimation, a dash of fey energy and a binding of elemental touches to the metal of the pen."

She could feel her power try to rise, but she held it in. His threatening display was waking all of her instincts, and her instincts were to pound him into the floor.

Tremble came up and snarled at the officer. "Remove your hand or I remove your arm."

Benny shifted when she was free and patted Tremble's arm. "Nice. You gave him a choice."

The necromancer glanced around for help and surprise flickered on his face when he noted that none of the day shift were on his side. The day shift was primarily made up of shifters and fey with a smattering of actual monsters. No one was going to help the officer against one of their own.

The duty agent came to them. "Anything else you need, Agent Ganger?"

"Nope. We are all checked out. She is in great shape. Well done." Benny grinned.

The duty agent nodded and smiled. "We do our best to keep them sane and alive."

Tremble put his arm around her waist and escorted her out of the building.

When they were inside the car and headed home, he turned to her. "What was that about?"

"What?"

"Seeing Jennifer, visiting Miaka?"

Benny looked at him and took in his obvious irritation. "Magic leaves a mark. It stamps those who have touched it or have been touched by it. Miaka is vulnerable, she needs to feel safe; Jennifer is unstable and losing her mind. She needs a tutor."

"You know a tutor for insanity?" He took one of her hands and stroked her palm with his thumb.

"No. I know a man who had to master his own development as a seer. He came into it as a teen and came up with techniques to manage his vision. He can teach Jennifer what she needs to know to keep her mind from being torn apart by the magic it is hunting for because of the residue of the imprint."

"Your father did that to her. Not you."

Benny sighed. "She was printed with my mind and aura. I know how she thinks. She doesn't trust anyone right now."

"You are still not stable. You are not recovered from your trip to the demon zone. I can feel it."

She sighed and gripped his hand. "I can rest when things are settled. I am pretty sure it will happen eventually."

He chuckled and leaned in to kiss her. The soft kiss of his lips quickly turned into something more heated and unsuitable for the front seat of a car.

When Pooky stopped moving and revved the engine, she reluctantly stopped the make-out session and yawned. "Time to catch up on more sleep."

They walked through the house and up the stairs, removing their clothing as quietly as they could. They settled in Tremble's bed, and he held her while they caught up on a bit more sleep.

She wished she hadn't finished her coffee.

Andrew hauled her out of bed and bullied her into the bathroom. "Come on, Benny. We need to eat and get to work in an hour. Don't want to be late."

She used the toilet and brushed her teeth again, brushing her hair into a more socially acceptable configuration that wouldn't frighten children before she left and retrieved her clothing.

Everybody was downstairs, and she heard the sounds of food being prepared when she went in search of her partners.

Omelettes were assembling in three skillets, and Andrew was watching them with a focused eye.

Tremble was checking his phone, and he smiled when she came into the kitchen. "We are going to be doing a road trip tonight."

Benny took the coffee that Argyle handed to her with a smile. "Where to?"

Tremble sighed. "We are doing a centaur transport. One of them manifested in a downtown club last night, so we are taking him to the preserve tonight."

She wrinkled her nose. "The one species I don't get along with."

The three men occupying her kitchen stared at her.

Andrew said, "You are kidding, right?"

"Nope. The magic that mixed the men and horses is a little too weird for me. I find the creepy." She shrugged and chuckled at their expressions. "Come on. There had to be a species I didn't get along with sooner or later."

Centaurs had a tendency to pursue females relentlessly, and it got tiring to be on guard all the time. She wanted to kill them and that wasn't a good frame of mind to be in for any period of time. It was even worse when murder was an actual option.

She smiled and leaned back as Argyle slid her plate in front of her. "Thanks."

He nodded. "Tremble mentioned that you had already visited Miaka and that you met with Jennifer."

She gave the elf a dark look. "Squealer."

"They needed to know."

She made a face and explained her reasoning for meeting with Jennifer. When she had detailed as much as she could, she sat and waited.

Andrew frowned. "Well, it doesn't seem that you did anything that would skew the case against your father. It should be fine."

Benny arched a brow. "You are a legal expert?"

He shrugged. "I dabble."

Argyle chuckled. "He was pre-law before he entered the XIA."

Andrew sighed. "Fine. I have studied law. But I have no idea how this case will turn out. There has never been another one like it. Demonic influence over infants is not a common occurrence."

Benny nodded and kept her mouth shut. The letter in the potion book had explained far more than she had ever imagined. If that knowledge could save her father from a life of incarceration, she would use it, but only if she had to.

They settled down to eat with Argyle supervising, and when the dishes were done, they set out to return to duty and haul a horse-boy off to the collective where other centaurs could control him.

*Yay.*

<h1 style="text-align:center">Chapter Nine</h1>

The centaur was named Steve, and he started making moves on her the moment he scented her. She didn't take it personally; he had also hit on the troll woman who had loaded him into the transport.

Since Steve got aggressive when any of the guys were around, it was Benny's duty to sit in the back of the transport with the shackled centaur and keep him calm.

"So, how many of those guys do you take at a time?" Steve shifted his hooves in their booted cuffs.

Benny sighed and glared at him. "One at a time. We don't need to pile onto each other to show affection."

He inhaled, and his sharply hooked nostrils flared. "You look human and smell like fey. Were you two doing each other before you had to pick me up?"

She gave him a bland look and whispered a small volume spell. He could still talk, but it was a tiny whisper.

"Benny, what is going on in there; I felt magic." Tremble's voice was a little nervous through the earpiece.

She chuckled. "Nothing. I just turned down the volume in here. It will return to normal when he is outside again."

"Okay. We did promise the colony that we would deliver him intact."

"I know. I won't neuter him. I promise. Tempting though it is."

"Great. Hang in there, Benny."

"Tremble, one more thing."

"What is it?"

"Are we there yet?"

His muffled snort sounded in her ear,

and she heard the others chortling in the background.

It was an hour later when the vehicle stopped moving and the sound of hoof beats approached the transport.

She waved the spell away and smiled. "Looks like this is your stop."

She felt power on the other side of the doors. Fey power.

Remembering what Jennifer had said, she let her control slip and let her body take what it recognised as its natural form.

A human-looking woman had stepped into the transport, a demon king walked out with the shocked centaur in tow. The trip down the ramp was slow, and she caught Steve when he stumbled, but he jerked away from her touch.

"Don't move away from a helping hand." She steadied him with a hand on his shoulder, and soon, they were on soft grass with a semi-circle of centaurs watching and a few lithe and pale fey in the background.

"What are you?"

She gave the appalled male a smirk. "Agent Ganger of the XIA."

The rest of her team was nearby, and they followed her lead, wrapping themselves in power.

Tremble waved to one of the men behind the centaurs, and the stunned elf made his way toward them.

"Cousin, it is good to see you."

Tremble inclined his head. "My prince. May I do you the honour of introducing my comrades?"

The elegant man who looked carved of moonlight smiled slightly. "I believe that would be wise as you are on our territory."

Introductions were made amongst the men, and finally, Benny faced Prince Emrick Brightleaf, ruler of the local lands.

He took her hand. "Beneficia Ganger? You cannot be. She has a human aspect."

Benny inclined her horned head. "I am indeed she. My aspect is what I wish it to be. I am currently displaying something more akin to my fey ancestors than is normally apparent."

Her words were slow and formal. She didn't want to flash the sharp teeth that didn't quite match the elegant deer horns.

"You are a woman with much power." His lips grazed her skin.

Smith stiffened next to her, but she accepted the caress.

"I am indeed. You are showing a remarkable lack of good sense, dear prince."

He raised his white eyebrows and smiled with his lips quirked to one side as he rose. "I am?"

"My partners are my partners in all things. As enchanting as your presence is, it will not be wise for the contact with you to continue."

He released her hand and took in the strange assembly. Smith had released Steve to the centaurs, and they had reluctantly left with their new member in tow.

Now, it was just the XIA and the fey.

Tremble moved to her side. "We were going to formally present ourselves, but we are joining in a union that is equal across our four bloodlines."

Prince Emrick could not have looked more shocked. "A union?"

"Married. The Ganger family is making the arrangements, but in our traditions, we were going to introduce ourselves to the fey community."

Benny blinked and smiled as her mind spun with the ramifications of this meeting. Normally, they would have started with the lowest members of the fey society and work their way to the prince if they had gained approval. Now, they only needed to get Emrick's authorisation and the rest had to follow.

"The Ganger family has authorised this union?" Prince Emrick was hesitant.

Benny inclined her head. "Yes. It is a little bulky, but hardly the strangest mating in my family line."

He looked ill at ease. "What of children?"

Ah, so that was it. "They will be raised as Gangers with the family affiliation made clear when paternity has been established. That will not be for a few years. I am enjoying my new life in the XIA. My family has never kept any distinctly blooded member from their people."

"In that case, I give you my blessing and await the invitation to the event. I am sure it will be a party to remember."

She inclined her head, and he backed away before slipping onto a horse that appeared from the shadows, and he and his party rode away.

She shook her head and resumed her human shape. "That was unexpected."

Benny held still as she was suddenly hugged from all sides.

Tremble was shaking as he held onto her. "You really mean to wed us all."

She caught on to what he said. She had changed them; they were no longer what they had been and their places in their own society were not assured.

"Of course. You are all Gangers now. You can even take the family name if you like. I am not fussy." She laughed as they kissed her in turn.

Finally, she called a halt. "We are on duty. Grab the boots and we will be on our way."

Argyle chuckled. "Ride next to me. I promise not to get grabby on the way home."

Benny leaned against him and sighed. "Sounds restful."

It was. The other two were busy trying to determine who would arrive at the altar first on the big day, and Benny had to throw a wrench into the works. "Smith, we still have to meet your alpha, and we need to meet Argyle's maker or king."

That thought seemed to shut him up for a while until they re-entered the city.

She dozed with her head against Argyle's shoulder until they pulled up to the XIA headquarters. Argyle's phone was in his hand, and he winked. "We have an hour."

She blinked. "What?"

"The king is waiting for us to present ourselves at his home. As this was our only assignment tonight, we are now free to attend at his pleasure."

Benny groaned. "We are so not

dressed for that."

Argyle opened the door and slid out, extending his hand to hers. "I am sure you will think of something."

After they were logged out and changed, she did indeed think of something and her companions' clothing was changed from denim into leather with a few choice bits of spell work.

Andrew sighed. "I suppose that my family is last."

Benny chuckled as Pooky took them through the calm and old neighbourhood where the vampire king mayor resided.

"You had a chance to pounce. You didn't pounce, so now we are going to see the vampires first." She wrinkled her nose at him as her clothing shifted around and under her in the car.

Pooky entered the long, sweeping drive, and Argyle spoke into the security camera, gaining them access to the surprisingly understated home.

"We are lucky in Mathias. He is a calm and understanding ruler." Argyle seemed to be making a point to both Tremble and Andrew.

When the car settled in front of the home, two shadows emerged from beside the doors to the house and stepped down to open their vehicle.

As Benny slid out of the car, her dress flowed into configuration around her—a leather overdress and trousers in contrasting black. Argyle took her hand, and they led the other two into the mayor's home.

Miss Leonora Wicks was waiting in the frame of the doorway as it opened at their approach. "Miss Ganger. I am delighted to see you again."

"Thank you, Leo. It is good to see you as well."

The woman still had the grey cast to her skin that had been there on their first meeting at the crime scene a few weeks earlier.

Once again, she smiled and her face went from blank and sober, to beautiful and welcoming. "He is waiting in the gardens. Your timing was perfect."

Argyle cleared his throat. "Allow me to introduce our bound companions."

Leo gave him another sweeping smile. "I don't care. This way."

She moved silently; her chiffon gown gave her the appearance of a floating spectre as they moved through the modest mansion and into the floral-scented darkness of the back garden.

The vampire king was tending his flowers and checking out his peach tree. "Leo, come here and taste this."

Miss Wicks rolled her eyes. "If I had a nickel for every time I heard that."

With a grin, the woman stepped toward the mayor, and he held out the fruit to her in a reverse of a biblical moment.

Benny watched as Leo reached for it with her hand, but Mathias held it so that she had to take it from his grip with her teeth.

Her face wasn't visible from that angle, but Benny knew that sound. Leo chewed furiously. "Not ripe!"

Mathias grinned and nodded. "I thought that was the case, but you know, I can't really tell."

Leo wrinkled her nose at him. "Your guests are here."

Mathias nodded and the peach arced through the air. Benny caught it and ripened it in her hand. She took a bite. "Thank you, Mayor Mathias."

He grinned. "It is good to see you again, Benny."

She released Argyle's hand and walked up to her family friend. "It is nice to see you so happy, Uncle Matt."

"It is good to feel it, Benny. Now,

what can I do for you and the good Argyle?"

Benny looked toward her vampire, and she smiled. "I wish to have him for my own, Uncle. We are bound, and now, I wish it to be formal in the eyes of the vampire nation."

"It will not be easy. He will outlive you if he does not suffer an injury."

She wrinkled her nose. "He is not quite one of yours anymore."

Mathias moved past her, and he grabbed Argyle by the chin and turned his head from side to side. "What did you do to him?"

Benny twisted her lips before biting into the peach again. "Nothing that he didn't consent to. They are mine; I am theirs; we are bound."

Mathias moved faster than she could track, examining Tremble and Smith as well. "All of them have a touch of demon in them."

"My blood."

Smith's teeth extended in surprise when the vampire king was suddenly in front of him. Mathias calmed him down.

"Easy, beast. I am just looking into...and there he is." Mathias looked into Tremble and nodded when he found the traces of Argyle he was seeking.

Benny blinked when Leo took the peach out of her hand and finished it. "Sorry. I had to get that sour taste out of my mouth."

A moment later, Mathias was next to her. "Well, you have given me three more subjects, so giving you one is fair enough."

Argyle came forward. "You are authorising our union?"

Mathias smiled. "Of course, Cairbre. I know what I am looking at and am both glad that I can call upon it and am willing to come if you call."

Leo took a call and walked into the

house; Mathias watched her go.

Benny looked from the doorway to the ancient power standing next to her. "Love?"

"As close as I can come. She has been through much, sacrificed much, and is always willing to give more. She is a woman to be admired, and I have not met one such as her before."

Benny nudged him with her arm. "Fire and ice under one skin."

He nodded. "Precisely. Now, dawn approaches and your companions look exhausted. Take them to bed."

She wrinkled her nose at him and gathered the men around her, ushering them back to Pooky and, from there, back home.

# Chapter Ten

As sweat dried on their bodies, Andrew asked her. "What exactly is passing between you and the heads of our clans?"

Their fingers were tangled together, and she rested her head against his shoulder. "Each one we speak to is acknowledging that your first duty is to our group, and each one knows that they are obligated to come to our defense, just as I am agreeing to come to their defense."

"I still don't get it."

"If your pride tangles with another, we will stand on the side of your pride, for the purpose of increasing numbers and to bring power. For Tremble's family, we bring fresh blood and energy, not to mention my family ties. That gives them added political clout when it comes to dealing with other principalities on the continent. They can get higher-ranking brides and husbands from other groups now."

"What do the vampires get?"

Argyle answered. "Protection. Protection from Benny's namesake. She can no longer hunt here unless Mathias requests it."

Benny yawned and snuggled against Andrew. "I am quite a catch."

Argyle reached out and patted her hip. "Yes, you are."

Tremble was reading a book across the room, and as she watched, he put the book down and crawled into bed.

She smiled as he curled around her. Given a choice, they preferred to be together. It was starting to feel like a family.

"Hey, Benny. We have a court date for an inquest." Her father's voice came through the phone as if he was next to her.

"When?" Benny finished brushing her teeth and held the phone to her cheek.

"Because of the publicity, we are going in tomorrow. They want to get everything settled and have me punished as quickly as they can." Harcourt laughed.

"You are sounding...better?"

"I am. The cut ties to Yomra have done wonders for my aspect. Your uncle Imriod is my counsel. I am sure things will turn out as well as they can."

"You know that they don't have call to be charging you."

"I know that they feel they have reason. The spell would have been passive if not for someone coming after you, but if you were not in danger, it would not have been needed.”

Benny nodded, though he couldn’t see her. “Right. Keep me posted. I want to be there.”

“I believe you are being named as a witness of some sort. You will be there, love.” She could hear the smile in his voice.

“Good. Glad that is out of the way.”

“Now, finish your teeth and get to work. We are hearing good things about how you are handling yourself.”

“You have spies watching me?”

“Of course. Just because you are an adult doesn’t mean we will stop trying to take care of you or make sure you are safe. It just means we do it from a distance. Have a good shift.”

The call was over in that light rush of speech, and she chuckled and spit out the foam. It was nice to know that she was still being cared for, even in her own place with her own family starting up. It was creepy, but nice, just like her parents.

Andrew was grilling ham steaks and Tremble was on waffles. Argyle was slicing fruit.

Benny checked her messages and texted a reply to Freddy that everything seemed to be going fine. Freddy demanded details, but Benny told her to get bent.

A plate slid in front of her, and she glanced up to see Andrew's smirk. "We have a half-hour appointment with my brother-in-law before work. Most of the pride won't be there, so it will be a little less tense than it would be on a weekend afternoon."

"Won't that be a little weird? I mean, it is usually a formal introduction for a mate from outside the pride."

"Well, when I mentioned that you had already met the other portions of our unit, he accelerated things to save face."

Tremble chuckled. "That shows he is more than an alpha; he is a politician."

Argyle nodded. "Very nice. Do you need us to do anything before we go?"

Andrew grinned. "Rub up against Benny and myself a few times. We still scent cue, so it will be faster if you smell like us."

Benny's fork froze halfway to her mouth as Argyle hugged Andrew without any delay. He stroked his cheek along the tanned skin of his partner, and Andrew's eyes closed for a moment.

When the embrace was over, Tremble stepped in and bent his head to repeat the caress on the other side of Andrew's face and neck.

The shudder that went through their lion was hard to miss.

Benny had to admit to being turned on by the sight of so much male muscle pressing together before parting. It was as if their clothing wasn't even there.

Argyle chuckled. "Benny. You might want to give us our shirts back."

She looked at him and blinked slowly. "Hmm?"

He lifted her free hand and pressed it to his cool, bare chest. "Shirts. Back."

She sat up and blushed. "Right. Sorry. Got caught up in the moment."

She sent the spell to clothe them through the air, and magic wrapped around them. Part of her sighed and kept replaying the scene over and over again. It was going into her foreplay memory file.

Benny made a mental note to figure out why her instincts had stripped them without any conscious direction. Unconscious magic could get dangerous very quickly.

She finished breakfast quickly and loaded the dishes into the dishwasher. Andrew pinned her against the counter.

"I just need your scent on me now." Andrew leaned in and brushed his cheek against hers.

Benny shook and reached up, looping her arms around his neck. "Done."

She leaned and pressed her lips to the column of his neck, exhaling against his skin.

He pressed firmly against her, and a low, rumbling purr sounded deep in his chest.

She nibbled, licked and stroked the hair at the back of his neck while she worked. When Andrew was vibrating under her touch, she relaxed and leaned back.

The husky tone in her voice was unmistakable as she said, "I believe we have an appointment with your alpha?"

His glare said a thousand words. "If he says one wrong thing, this is going to get very ugly."

The guys jostled each other as they

headed for the door; the XIA would be their first stop, to check on Miaka and then the trip to Andrew's family seat would be next.

Spirits were high, but there was an underlying tension that hadn't been there before.

Miaka was sitting with a notebook and a necromancer when Benny arrived.

The necromancer got to her feet and smiled. "Good afternoon, Agent Ganger. I have heard wonderful things about you."

The woman extended her hand, and Benny reached out to shake it. The contact was a little startling, but the shock of cold didn't stop Benny from shaking the hand of the self-animating woman in front of her.

"I am glad to know it. You have the advantage of me."

"Ah, I am Kima Remiller. I specialise

in instructing those who have specific talents, like Miaka here. I will be her private tutor during her time in the restricted facility, and when she is released, she will join us at a school specialising in the arts of the undead."

Benny released Kima's hand and glanced over at Miaka. "You have been sentenced?"

She nodded, and Michael gave a thumbs-up behind her head. "I was sentenced under the magical-stress provision. Michael testified for me. Your statement on the matter carried some weight."

Benny paused before she realised that Miaka was referring to the report she had written in the car and the follow-up report when they had brought Miaka into the XIA.

"I am glad it helped. Grief can make folk do extraordinary things."

Kima nodded wisely. "It can indeed.

She has a lot of potential, and it needs to be directed so that she and society can feel the benefit."

Benny felt an unfurling sense of relief. She couldn't hug Miaka, but she patted her on the shoulder and promised to keep in touch as much as was feasible.

Kima sat down again, and they continued their lesson with both Michael and Miaka paying close attention. It was yet another wonderful mental image to walk away with.

Today was turning into quite an encouraging day.

"So, Dornan will come out of the house with my sister, Emily. The betas might be behind them, and the attached alphas will be outside on guard. Everybody will be watching Dornan. If he goes on alert, we will all be in for it." Andrew spoke grimly.

Argyle had his sunglasses on, and he

glanced over at Andrew. "What happens if he goes on alert?"

Andrew sighed. "We will have to fight for our place in the pride."

Tremble grinned. "Do we want a place in the pride?"

Benny elbowed him. "Shush. Of course. This is even all the way around. Elves, vamps and now lions. Everybody is going to have all the backup we can manage."

Tremble took her hand and raised it to his lips. "Yes, Benny."

Andrew turned down the long drive and jerked his head toward the sprawling ranch house with high spires at every corner. "Felines love a high perch. We are no exception. They saw us on the highway. You can see them gathering on the grounds and emerging from the woods. Huh. There are more off today than I thought."

Benny didn't comment that it didn't

seem to be a good thing. A yard full of lion shifters was setting her senses on edge.

Argyle was flexing his hands, and Tremble's ears were as alert as she had ever seen them. Even Andrew was on alert.

Meeting a swirling and evolving family was definitely different from the cold greeting of the fey and the relaxed moments with the vampires. Benny braced for anything.

Andrew pulled in at a safe distance from the house, and he glanced at them. "Okay, you have been briefed and we are all ready for a fight. I don't think that there is anything else to cover."

Benny nodded. "We are going to follow your lead, Andrew. We are going to take our cues from you."

"Got it. Well, here we go."

In a rehearsed move, three of them opened their doors while Benny unbuckled. When they gathered outside her door, Andrew opened it and took her hand to guide her out. She was the alpha female to their gathering of alphas, and they were exhibiting their protection. It was odd, but since the lionesses owned the property, they were entitled to protection. Benny was their ersatz lioness.

They stepped toward the front doors of the home and paused a safe distance from the threshold. The doors opened, and Dornan and Emily came out, with Emily's heavy belly leading the way.

Dornan gave a formal nod. "Andrew You bring members of your pride here to greet us?"

Andrew jerked his head slightly. "I have. They are my pride and my family. I would like to introduce you."

Emily nodded her head. "Come, brother. I need a hug and your nieces are going out of their heads waiting until this is safe."

Andrew nodded and stepped forward. "Dornan Bearing, Emily Smith-Bearing, I would introduce you to my partners. Tremble, Argyle and Agent Ganger are my chosen life bonds. They are my family and now yours."

Dornan stepped forward, and they could feel the eyes on them from every angle. He walked up to Andrew and inhaled the scent off his body. He shuddered slightly and then came over to greet them in precisely the same ways.

Emily came up behind him and repeated the actions, rubbing Benny's cheek with her own in greeting. Tension eased and everyone relaxed. The members of the pride slowly walked in to greet and accept the newcomers in their midst. One small moment turned from tense to warm, and it made Benny smile.

Emily pulled her aside as the little girls rushed out to meet their new uncles and aunty. "I think he is where he is supposed to be."

Benny watched Andrew move through his family and pride members accepting congratulations for his bravery and the power that his new pride exhibited.

"I think so, too. We just all fit. The odds were against it, but there it is. We fit together and nowhere else."

Argyle had a three year old on his shoulders and Tremble was holding the toddler with aplomb.

Emily linked arms with her, indicating her instant comfort. "I think they would make great fathers."

"I think so, too, but I am waiting until I have a few years in the XIA under my belt. We have joined more than lodgings; we have linked lifespans. I have a bit more time than most humans are granted."

"So, you are thinking of having kids?" Emily tried to be sly.

"Of course. Tremble has already volunteered to be the house husband, but none of us are in a rush. We can't be. We have no idea who the father of the first would be."

Emily blushed. "So you.. all together?"

"No. But it is fairly serial. One sets off the others and so on."

A sly female voice from behind Benny murmured, "It sounds like a circus."

Emily stiffened and turned with Benny. "Maggie, you were not invited to speak."

The woman was beautiful, golden and had the sly look of an ex-girlfriend.

If Benny didn't have such a good opinion of her own worth as a female, she would have been intimidated. As it was, she smiled slightly and extended her hand. "Pleased to meet you."

Maggie narrowed her eyes and sneered. "I don't shake hands with mongrels."

Emily's shoulders stiffened. "You are speaking to my soon-to-be sister-in-law."

"Madam Alpha, you are going to have to choose between pride and family. You can't have both. Eric deserves better."

Benny lowered her hand; her brain was smug in the knowledge that Maggie didn't call him Andrew. That was the name he preferred, and if she didn't use it, she didn't know him all that well.

Benny smiled. "He does deserve better. He chose better. He has three loyal partners, and we would all fight to the death for him."

Maggie's features shifted for battle, and she lunged forward. "Prove it."

# Chapter Eleven

$\mathcal{B}$enny shifted to keep Emily out of the line of attack, and she let her other form out.

The half-shifted, charging lioness's eyes widened in shock as she was facing a demon king with fey eyes and vampire calm.

It was almost comical to see the woman go from aggressive to grovelling as Benny grabbed her, flipped her and pinned her to the ground with one hand in her hair and her head back. It was a submission pose and Maggie didn't fight it.

Emily cleared her throat. "Well, that was unexpected."

Benny looked at her new sister. "Apologies. I had hoped to ease you into this particular manifestation."

Emily waved it off. "Not you. Them."

Benny looked over to where the guys were standing and the demon manifestations were exceedingly obvious.

"What did you do to my brother?"

Benny wrinkled her nose. "We are all bound together. It was necessary, but we now share portions of all the others in our odd little unit. The demon manifestation is me, fey is Tremble, and Argyle's teeth and calm come in handy. We get enhanced senses and claws from Andrew."

Emily hugged her belly. "All that is just inside you?"

Benny held Maggie in the twisted position and smiled. "Of course. I only let it out on special occasions. It was important for Andrew's family to know what we had become, together."

Emily exhaled. "Well, you don't seem like a ravening beast, and you don't seem evil."

Benny didn't mention that she wanted to snap Maggie's neck as casually as you would swat a fly. She smiled and looked down at her prisoner. "Are you going to behave?"

Maggie nodded slowly and as much as should was able to. "Yes."

Benny whispered a charm to lock Maggie in her half-shifted form for a day. "Now, you are going to have to deal with having your furry face on display for a day. Twenty-four hours from now, you will regain control. Never attack me or mine again. It is not worth your life to try and gain position by aggression."

Maggie scuttled back the moment that Benny let her go.

Benny looked at Emily and slowly receded back into her normal skin. It was a little disturbing that it was coming so easily when she wanted extra power. Reaching for her demon side wasn't her favourite means of defense.

Andrew came up to her and wrapped her in his arms. "Are you all right?"

She nodded. "I am fine. She didn't lay a claw on me."

Maggie was sitting on the ground with her hands on her face, her claws a little too near her eyes for Benny's liking.

Emily sighed. "I will look after her. Thank you for not killing her."

Benny nodded toward Emily. "It was a near thing...wait how did you know?"

He chuckled and rubbed his chin on the top of her head. "When you change, we can feel what you feel through our binding. It is definitely not the way we imagine you normally think. It is far more aggressive."

She sighed. "Sorry."

Dornan cleared his throat. "Well,

since I have seen the power that you bring to our pride, welcome once again, Beneficia Ganger."

She gave Andrew a quick look before turning in his arms and opening his embrace.

"We bring you power, allies and magic. What does your pride offer us?"

Dornan blinked. "We offer you companionship, allies and family."

Benny stepped forward. "Right answer. Welcome to the family, Alpha."

He bent his head, and they rubbed cheeks for a moment. He smelled like dry oak leaves and musk with a hint of sunshine.

"Welcome, sister."

"Thank you, brother." Benny smiled and returned to Andrew's embrace, tucking his arms around her. They had some time to formally meet the rest of the available pride, but then, work called. Benny was looking forward to taking on the minutia of the XIA. Tomorrow was going to be stressful, so she wanted to bury herself in the boring details of extra-natural law enforcement.

When a little girl tapped at her leg demanding an introduction, Benny grinned. She was now an aunty. Today was definitely a distraction.

Back in the SUV, Benny enjoyed the sucker that little Melody had given her. Benny had responded by enchanting a few strands of braided grass into a flower that would change its appearance every six hours. The little girl had hugged her and immediately taken off to show every lion on the premises her new flower.

Andrew chuckled. "I am getting all kinds of ideas watching you with that sucker."

She opened her mouth and crunched down on the candy.

Three voices said, "Ouch."

Argyle had a strange expression not accounted for by her candy assassination.

"Argyle, what's up?"

He smiled slightly. "I haven't been out like this in actual daylight in an extremely long time."

He had been wearing a hood that sat on his shoulders at the moment, but his skin hadn't burned or even heated up. Even his eyes didn't show their normal irritation from the sun.

"Oh. I am guessing you have gotten better?"

He grinned. "I got something."

Tremble chuckled. "You sound like it is an STD."

They all laughed at that.

Argyle shrugged. "I suppose I will have to get used to being nearly human again, so to speak."

Benny smiled. "Consider it adjusting

to daylight and leave it at that. I don't think any of us qualify for human anymore."

Tremble snorted. "I never was human, nor was Andrew."

Andrew turned and gave Tremble a look. "I was for a few years. I mean I was raised in the pride, but shifting didn't kick in until puberty."

Argyle cleared his throat. "I was twenty-six. I was human. I remember human. I don't know what to do with it now."

Benny blinked. "If you want it changed, I am sure that we could supress the humanity."

He shook his head. "No. I am just wondering where the nearest beach is."

The occupants of the vehicle chuckled and pulled into the XIA. In ten minutes, they were logged in, changed and armed for the evening. The skies were red and the shenanigans were about to start.

Benny cuffed the nymph that had been seducing her way through the park in an effort to find her way home. It was an odd means of location, but it worked for nymphs. Someone would eventually help her get home.

The boys had to hang back on this one. The nymph could seduce simply by looking into a man's eyes. Benny was going to have to hang onto her until the collection wagon arrived.

"This isn't really fair." Benny kept her grip on the nymph while the others interviewed participants in the unlawful sex acts. They were all going to get a summons to appear.

Tremble shrugged. "Sorry. It is you or us. I think your odds at resisting her are greater."

Benny snorted and waited for the pick-up.

Two female officers were driving the

collection vehicle tonight. One of the females was a porcupine shifter, and she wasn't going to take any guff from a lonely nymph looking for directions. It was the public sex that had been the problem, all six times.

Benny made sure that her charge was tucked away and her cuffs were retrieved before the transport left.

"Are you guys finished with your gawking?"

Tremble shrugged. "You are best suited to dealing with females with seduction on their minds."

She snorted and winked as she slid into the passenger seat to type in an incident report. "I thought that was your job."

Argyle leaned against the doorframe next to her. "Only when we are allowed to act on it and only with you."

Agent Smith got behind the wheel. "He isn't wrong. Aside from the enjoyment your wrestling with the nymph provided, it was your body we wanted."

Blushing and concentrating were difficult things to do at the same time, but she managed to get the report details down to the transport vehicle number and agent designations.

"Right. Done. What's next?"

Argyle cleared his throat. "Since I am riding shotgun today, let me check."

She blushed and got out of the passenger seat and waved him in. "Apologies, Agent Argyle."

He stroked her arm and settled in his position. Benny scampered around the car and headed for her position behind the driver.

A moment later, they were in motion and Argyle was sending them to the park where they had entered the demon zone. Apparently, the goblin fires were still burning.

Tremble gave her a side-glance.

"What can we do about the goblin fires?"

Benny shrugged. "We will see when we get there."

Argyle looked at her. "What does that mean?"

She wrinkled her nose. "I said we will see. I can't guess until I see the actual blazes. I do know we need to go out with fangs and claws."

Smith glanced at her in the rear view mirror. "Why?"

"Goblins only pay attention if you are scary. It is what they are wired for. Demon aspects are too scary, so we just need to be pointy."

Everyone in the car chuckled. It seemed that the demon aspects were something that they were getting used to. It would set them apart for the rest of their lives, but now, they were apart, together.

# Chapter Twelve

Benny checked her watch, and at the minute mark, she stepped into the flames. Around the park, her team did the same.

*Ah, mistress, what do you wish of me?*

*Oh, fire djinn, element of the burning desert, we wish for you to cease your flickering flame and take yourself to where the population isn't.*

The focus of the wish was the important thing. When you dealt with magical, living flame that you had only read about in books, it was best to stick to the formalities.

*This place provides plenty of magic*

---

*and a new wave of it is nearly upon us. I like it here.*

*You are disturbing the population and frightening children. They do not know what or who you are. There is no place for you here.*

The flame wreathed her hands and arms. *Where will I go? It was magic that summoned me here.*

From across the park, Benny felt an idea blossom in Argyle's mind.

*I accept your offer.*

*What? What offer?*

*To reside at your home until the wave comes and I can take a body again.*

The flame rose up, and the dozens of fires across the park wove together into a column that swirled away and streaked through the sky.

Benny knelt on the scorched ground and caught her breath. Her fumbling hand pulled out her phone, and she made a quick call.

"Hiya, Mom."

Her mother's voice was amused. "Hello, Benny."

"Argyle offered our family property to a fire djinn as a resting place. It is on the way."

"It is already here, Benny. He is very polite and has accepted the ruin at the back of the property as his domain for the time being."

"That was quick."

"He is fire, Benny. He moves quickly."

She paused, "Are you ready for to-morrow night?"

Her mother sighed. "They are offering me immunity from prosecution as an accessory if I testify against him."

"Are you going to take it?"

"Your father wants me to, and he has that look in his eyes that he knows something I don't, so I think I will."

"Good. Well, I had better get back to

work. Take care of our new companion."

Her mother laughed. "I will use him to clear the poplar cluster at the back of the property."

"Thanks, Mom. Night."

"Night, baby."

Benny hung up, put her phone away and got back to her feet. The other three were staggering toward her.

Smith shook his head. "Why am I so tired?"

Tremble answered him, "Because all of your body heat was consumed by the djinn. I have never met one before, but it was just as described."

Argyle looked from one of them to the other. "Shouldn't that have killed you?"

Benny studiously brushed dirt from her knees.

Three voices said, "Benny?"

She looked at her nails and then flicked glances at them. "It was Tremble's contribution to our group. Fey are immune to the effect of the djinn."

Tremble blinked. "What?"

Benny wrinkled her nose. "I will show you the book when we get home. There is a reason that fey are in my family line; aside from being pretty, you are surprisingly sturdy."

Tremble blushed, and they all returned to the vehicle. Argyle gestured for Benny to sit behind the computer. "I have no idea how to describe what we just did."

She settled in behind the computer and started typing. "Big words from the guy who offered to let a djinn settle in our back yard."

"I don't know why I suggested that."

She chuckled and patted his shoulder. "He planted the idea. Djinn are known to grant wishes, but most of those wishes are their own."

Argyle watched the words flow from her tapping fingers, and he chuckled as she outlined the very basics of what had occurred, including requesting the elemental being to leave. She did not fill in the departure details or where it was currently located.

When she was done, she sent the report and slid past Argyle, patting him on the arm. She wanted desperately to kiss him, but they were on duty.

She settled in her spot and leaned back with her eyes closed as they started moving.

A hand shook her gently, and the scent of tacos brought her all the way around. Benny sat up and blinked at Tremble's face.

"Come on, Benny. This should wake you up. We had him make it to your standard requirements."

Benny moved slowly and exited the vehicle, leaning on Tremble as he supported her to the picnic tables in the empty lot.

Argyle and Smith were waiting and drawing a bit of a crowd. Apparently, the locals were not yet used to XIA agents finding their little out-of-the-way taco truck.

Tremble supported her to the seat, and Argyle slid the tacos practically under her nose. She picked up her first target and started to eat.

Smith and Tremble started in on their own food, and Argyle kept watch over the whispering crowd.

Benny barely registered the food as she made her way into her serving. Normally, she should have been sweating, but her guess was that the djinn took more heat than she had been aware of. She was in thermal shock.

She had no sooner realised it than Tremble pressed against her left side and Smith on her right. Argyle didn't have any body heat to contribute.

When she finished four brain-meltingly hot tacos, Tremble got her a refill. She kept eating until the final drop of grease hit the paper. Warmth was returning.

She drank her peppered soda and sighed. "Thanks. I needed that."

Tremble nudged her with his thigh. "We could feel it."

"It was probably why the djinn left so suddenly. He knew he had taken too much." Smith's voice was grim.

She nodded. "Probably."

"It is nearly dawn. We were in that fire for three hours."

Benny groaned and flexed her hands. "That would explain it."

Tremble nudged her again. "The captain wants to speak with us before we go off shift."

She nodded and balled up the remains of the food wrappers. "Ready when you are."

Argyle tidied up, and they headed back to the vehicle.

No one spoke during their trip. Benny suspected that the meeting had to do with her family troubles, but she couldn't be sure until they actually talked to Matheson.

The XIA was surprisingly calm when they arrived. They made it through security and were knocking on the captain's door without anyone speaking to them.

When "Come in" sounded, they walked into the office where four chairs were arranged in front of the captain's desk. He was sitting and scribbling notes in a book.

"Good. Sit."

Bemused, they took seats with Benny sitting across from the captain and the others to the left and right with Argyle nearest the door.

The captain leaned back in his chair and sighed. "Your little team is weird but effective, even for the XIA."

They waited.

"With Agent Ganger's parents' inquest beginning tomorrow, I am afraid that that effectiveness will be compromised during the proceedings. You are suspended from active duty until the matter is closed."

Smith leaned forward. "Why?"

The captain grimaced. "It is a demand from the administrators. If you are on active duty and something is disseminated during the inquest, you may be at risk, and if anyone attacks you, the risk will transfer to them. It is to protect the public as well as your team."

Benny wrinkled her nose. "Didn't we already do this?"

Captain Matheson chuckled. "We did, and we will do it again if it is necessary. I want you focused on the job. The team is getting amazing results, and it has caused the mages to consider offering a few of their staff members to us while you are gone. I had no idea that you were a member of the guild."

She scratched her chin. "I had inherited membership. I was a Mage Guide when I was younger, and apparently, that is a gateway to full guild status. I never bothered pursuing it as I would have had to have formal education in the magical arts."

He gave her a surprised look.

She pointed at her chest. "When it came to magic, I was home schooled. No diploma, so no guild status."

He nodded. "Right. Well. That aside, you have made enough of an impression in their magical circles to get us additional staff, so we are not going to be shorthanded while you are on leave."

Tremble cocked his head. "Is there any idea how long this leave will be?"

Matheson shrugged. "That is up to the courts, but I don't want you back until Agent Ganger's family is stable in whatever position that they settle. Guilt or innocence will be determined, and we will arrange matters after we know how the public has reacted."

Benny felt the emotions running through the binding that held them together. She didn't say anything.

Tremble cleared his throat. "If the public comes out against Benny, what happens then?"

Matheson rubbed the back of his neck. "We will deal with it if it happens. I cannot guess what is being planned for you, but there are options being considered, no matter what the court decides."

Benny nodded tightly. "Wonderful. Well, I suppose that is that."

"You are hereby dismissed on suspension of duties with full pay." Captain Matheson nodded. "Use the time wisely."

Argyle nodded and got to his feet. He

extended his hand to Benny, and the others got up as well. There was nothing else to say.

They headed to the change room and got back into their civilian clothing.

Benny's mood was dark as they headed to the parking lot, but when Tremble exclaimed in delight, she smiled. Pooky had brought some friends. Pooky was standing in equine form with three horses of the Wild Hunt in full view of all the XIA and two reporters who were nearby.

Argyle smiled and escorted her to her steed. "Well, this will be interesting."

When they were all mounted and smirking foolishly, the beasts wheeled and galloped across the lot and down the highway in a heady beat of hooves. The number of flashes that had caught them as they rode out meant that they were going to be appearing in some sort of news report in the next day.

Benny enjoyed the wind in her hair and the feel of Pooky under her. They reached speeds that a normal vehicle would have had trouble keeping up with, until they thundered into the wide meadow behind the dower house.

Tremble's eyes were glowing, and his hair was a wild wave down his back. Argyle looked like a blood king, and Smith's own gleaming golden skin was alive with the last of the night. Even Benny felt more awake and encouraged by the gallop through the night.

When the steeds pulled up, even with the dower house, Tremble dismounted and walked toward her, putting his hands on her waist and pulling her over his shoulder. Instead of heading toward the house, he strode into the woods, and she only caught a glimpse of the other two heading for the house.

Her clothing turned into a silk robe, and he tore the silk down the centre as he lifted her to a tree. The bark went from rough to silken against her back while he pinned her and moved into her with energy.

Benny surrendered to her senses, and when Tremble shouted his release, her power joined his and spread through the forest in waves.

She was holding tight to his shoulders, and the pearl of his skin gleamed in the last shreds of moonlight. Her heart was thudding in her chest, and she fought to get her breath.

Tremble pressed soft kisses to her shoulder and up her neck. Benny smiled and threaded her fingers through the loose mane of his hair. "You need to go for a ride more often."

He grinned against her neck. "You will always be my favourite steed."

Her giggle rippled through the forest, and she heard a laughing answer in the trees.

"Uh oh."

He raised his head. "What?"

"Why did you pick the forest?"

He frowned. "It was close."

"Was it, or did something call you?"

She unlocked her legs and tried to slide down his body, but he caught her before she could touch the mossy ground. A silken robe wrapped around him and hers reformed to cover her.

Tremble held her against him so that her feet still didn't touch the ground. "Why are you worried?"

"I think we may be waking something. The whispers in the woods are turning into laughter. Something in there is excited."

He smiled and stroked her cheek. "I think that was us."

She frowned and smacked his arm. "Something else. I can hear it."

He nuzzled her cheek. "I can hear it as well. Don't worry about it. It isn't harmful. The woods here have just gotten old enough to have a dryad. The forest here is in labour. It needs more power to bring her out."

"Uh, how long is that going to take?"

"A few decades."

Benny raised her head. "What?"

"What we just did was an early contraction. The labour is just starting."

"Do you know which tree it is?"

He grinned. "Not yet. We will all be invited when it is time."

"So, I am guessing that we are now tied to the land."

He swung her fully into his arms and carried her across the meadow. "You manifest as a forest lord in your demon form and you are only now accepting your tie to the land? I thought you were smarter than that."

She smacked his chest, and he chuckled all the way to the house. The sounds of clanking weights told her what the other two were up to. While Tremble had worked his invigoration off with her, they had chosen the ancient method of physical exertion.

Tremble carried her up the stairs and cuddled with her in the bizarrely large bed. It was still going to take some getting used to, but when he curled around her and held her against him, she was willing to try.

A few hours later, hands on her body and a blindfold over her eyes wakened her. She tried to determine who was touching her by the temperature of their skin. After a few minutes, she gave up trying to figure out what was who, and she simply enjoyed it.

If this was what suspension had in store for her, she hoped that her parents took up a life of petty crime after the inquest.

# Chapter Thirteen

"Harcourt Emile Ganger, we are here to determine whether charges should be laid on you for the soul interference with eight infants thirty years ago."

The occupants of the chamber murmured, but Benny sat with her partners in silence. Her mother was sitting in the row ahead of her, and her father was in a separate section, under guard.

The judge finished the explanation of why everyone was there and sat back. "Prosecution, proceed to make your case."

The prosecution stood up and outlined the case. Benny had been born and her parents had been worried about her. Her father had crept to the nursery and copied her aura and soul on to the other baby girls.

It was that selfish act to defend his own daughter that had led Harcourt Emile Ganger into the path of endangering the newborns that were next to her. That danger had come to roost in the last two years, resulting in seven deaths.

The use of demonic energy in the alteration of the life patterns of eight babies was the charge. Using them as bait carried a relatively minor sentence, but the soul tampering was the major infraction.

Jennifer was called as a witness to the assault due to her imprint of Benny's patterns.

"He grabbed me and I don't remember much after that. The energy felt weird and greasy. I vaguely heard shouting, but I didn't wake until I was in hospital. I had no idea why I had been marked for death until I was briefed by my parents' counsel." Jennifer looked more rested than she had the last time they ran into each other.

The prosecutor nodded. "What did you think about what had been done to you?"

"I was shocked. I have always enjoyed a normal if oddly successful life. To hear that the way I think was a copy of someone else...it was a shock." Jennifer swallowed.

The prosecutor nodded sympathetically. "Understandable. Has it impacted your life?"

"Before, I don't know. But after the imprint was removed, I definitely felt different. My brain has changed."

"So, the trauma has sent you into a downward spiral?"

Jennifer sat up and blinked. "No. It just changed my direction. I am doing much better now."

Benny tried not to crack a smile, but she felt her lips twitch. Her smirk faded as the prosecutor listed the names of the dead women.

Each of the women had lived full and vibrant lives. None had a husband or child and all were at the top of their field.

Finally, the prosecutor pointed out that even Harcourt's wife was willing to speak against him. He couldn't bring up the demon issue as Benny's dad was firmly in control of his human form once again.

The prosecutor rested their petition.

"I now call the defense to make the case to deny a court date." The judge nodded.

The defense counsel got to his feet and cleared his throat. "I call Beneficia Ganger to the stand, as per my client's request."

Benny got up and sat in the witness box, facing the families of the deceased and her parents. Her mom smiled weakly and waved briefly. Benny inclined her head.

"Beneficia Ganger, do you swear to tell the truth in this matter?" The gargoyle snapped his wings, and she focused on him.

"I do so swear."

The counsel brought out a glowing orb. "Do you agree to hold this orb for the entire portion of questioning?"

She knew that orb. It would sting like hell if she lied. "I do."

The orb was placed in her palms, and she balanced her hands on the edge of the box in front of her.

"What is your relation to this case?"

Benny blinked. "Oh, I am Beneficia Ganger, the daughter of Harcourt and Lenora Ganger. I was the baby that they made the copy of."

The orb tingled.

"That they copied the signature of."

"Why did they do this?"

She inhaled and exhaled before stating it for the record. "I come from a family with demon bloodlines, and my mother's bloodline had its own power. My parents wanted to protect me, so since they couldn't hide my birth, they hid my location."

The gargoyle smiled. "Your father doesn't seem like a demon."

"We have only recently cut the ties that bind our family to the patriarch of our bloodline. It has caused a ripple effect in all of us, but now, my dad looks like he did when I was little."

"What do you mean? How did he change?"

Benny twisted her lips. "Which time are you referring to? I want to be precise."

"The first time. When did he change

and why?"

Benny cleared her throat. "He changed when my mother died. He had to take on his demon form to bring her back. He didn't regain a human form until recently."

The gargoyle nodded, "So, the statement from the nurse that a male demon came into the nursery and bewitched her could not have been an accurate statement of events from three decades ago."

Benny chuckled. "No. He looked just like he does now. We have family pictures, school pictures and articles from the universities where he used to teach. His green and scaly form didn't manifest until after my mother's illness."

The judge was making notes and he asked the prosecution, "How did the nurse identify the defendant?"

The prosecutor scowled. "From a lineup of demon photos."

The judge nodded. "Thank you."

The defense attorney nodded his head and asked, "You said you had demon blood. How does it manifest for you?"

"I am strong, fast and can access magic across all boundaries."

"Do you have a demon shape?"

"I got one recently, yes."

"May we see it?"

"I do not see how it is pertinent to what we are here for."

The judge nodded. "Please oblige."

Benny shrugged and she shifted. A few humans and mages recoiled, but far more leaned forward, fascinated. There were not many chances to see a demon in public.

"Now, can you tell me what you did when you came upon the form of Jennifer Langstrom?"

"After we drove off the murderer, I removed the template on her mind. I had just learned of the serial murders and had located Jennifer via my ride along with the XIA."

"Were you with them when they figured out she was in danger?"

Benny bit her lip. "I was the one who figured out what was going on once my parents told me about the other babies. I told the XIA, and we all worked to track and find the remaining woman. We found her just in time."

"Who was hunting her?"

Benny had to be honest. "No one. They were hunting me. My great-grandfather, the demon king Yomra had manipulated a human into killing the women in an effort to concentrate my power."

The gargoyle blinked. "What? What do you mean?"

"The spell that was cast on the babies wasn't a demon construct, it was a soul split. The girls each became part of me, and when they died, those parts came flooding back."

"Didn't you notice?"

Benny blushed. "I thought I had finally finished puberty."

The courtroom erupted in laughter and snickers. Even Harcourt laughed.

When the room was quiet again, the gargoyle asked, "Your mother offered her testimony against her husband in this case and received full immunity for it. Do you know why that would be?"

"Because she knows he didn't do it."

"How do you know that?"

"Because I know who did."

The prosecutor got to his feet. "Objection."

The judge tapped his desk. "This is an inquest, not a trial. Object all you like, we are still hearing it."

The gargoyle smiled. "Now, Miss Ganger, who did this terrible deed?"

Benny looked at her mom and smiled. "My mother."

Lenora gave her a thumbs-up.

The courtroom was in an uproar again, and the gallery shifted restlessly. The judge called a halt to the inquest, and a recess with the public banned from the resumption of the proceedings. It didn't sit well, but the courtroom was cleared via a herding spell. She handed the gargoyle the orb and returned to her people.

Benny was wrapped in Tremble, Argyle and Smith as the crowd pushed in. She belatedly shifted back to human and held onto Smith's back as he used his broad shoulders to keep them from the crowd.

Tremble whispered, "How long have you known?"

"The binding spell. My mom put a confession between the pages of her potion book, thinking that she would be dead before I ever found it. Dad never brews potions, so he wasn't able to destroy it. When she came back from hospital, she was missing a few months before her stay there, so I am guessing she never knew that she confessed."

The defense counsel met them outside the doors and escorted them to a small waiting room with guards to make sure that no one spoke to the attorneys.

The break was only fifteen minutes, but it was enough time for Benny to cuddle up to each of her partners and relax in their embrace.

Argyle whispered, "You are doing great, Benny."

She smiled, and when the bell chimed, they filed back to the courtroom, which was now exceedingly empty.

The judge gestured for Benny to retake the witness box, and the orb was back in her hands.

The attorney fluttered his wings and cleared his throat. "You had just stated that your mother was the one who had cast the spell in the hospital nursery."

"I did."

"Why should we believe that you are not simply trying to save your father as you share your demon nature with him?"

She held up the orb. "This object was created to shock anyone who is telling what their mind acknowledges as an untruth."

"Demons lie."

She cocked her head. "They don't actually; they simply act in their own best interests and pursue their own pleasure. They lack a conscience, not common sense. And I am only partially demon. I have far more fey in me than I do demon blood, but no one is commenting on the rainbow eyes."

"Why do you think that your mother cast the spell?"

Benny quirked her lips. "She wanted to hide me and to keep my power at a reasonable level. The splitting of my power managed it. With only a trickle of demon energy, all of those girls grew up with bright minds and a drive to learn and succeed. It defied their upbringing in several cases."

"How are you so aware of them?"

She blinked. "After I learned they existed, I wanted to find their points of commonality. I researched them after they had passed on. Jennifer is the only one I have seen in person."

He nodded and checked his notes. "You mentioned that your mother had passed. Is this your stepmother?"

"No. She is the one who bore me, wiped my nose and applied first aid when I did something stupid. That happened a lot."

The orb remained stubbornly quiet, and Benny settled in for a long interrogation.

Chapter Fourteen

$\mathcal{B}$enny filled in about her parents and home life growing until the moment her mother got ill.

"I don't like to speak of it, but she lost a few months of memory after she came home. She recovered, but never got the memory of the worst time of her illness back."

"Were there any other changes at that time?"

"Dad turned green and scaly with horns. Is that enough?"

"Thank you, Miss Ganger. You may return to your seat."

Benny got up and handed him the orb on her way down. She resumed her seat with Argyle on one side and Smith on the other.

The defense spoke to her dad. "Mister Ganger, how is it that the soul of your daughter came to be split into nine pieces?"

The gargoyle handed the orb over to Harcourt. He sighed.

"I had marking to do for my class, and I went home to finish it so I could get back to the hospital to be with my wife and daughter. At that time, I was teaching at two local universities and consulting at five colleges." He sighed and ran a hand through his hair.

"Lenora was agitated when I left. It had not been an easy birth, and Benny had not been strong when she made it into the world. Lenora was worried, and I left her anyway." He flexed his hands and his face showed his regret.

"When I came back, she was in bed, her hands tight together and her lips white. She said she had done what she had to, to protect our baby. Benny was safe and her godmother would look after her if Lenora didn't make it. I told her she was being silly, but she was haunted. We brought Benny home, and Lenora got better, but I always remembered what she had said. She had kept them from finding her so Benny would be safe." Harcourt's voice broke and he gather himself.

"When she was dying, she told me what she had done. I had told her I was worried about Benny's slow development in the magical arts. With us as her parents, I was expecting her to show more power at an earlier stage. The spell for division of power explained it all. Benny could get by on one-ninth of the power she was born with, and the others would benefit greatly."

The attorney nodded. "What happened to your wife?"

"She got cancer, and there was nothing that we could do. We had to wait until it ran its course, and then, I was able to put demon magic to use. Unfortunately, using the magic left the stain on my body."

"What did you do?"

"I used demon venom to key her to my body and burned the cancer out of her body. I brought her back using the control I had to spark her life, and from there, her own magic took over. I lost my human aspect, but I kept my love."

"Did you resume teaching?"

"No. Lenora and I continued consulting as researchers, but we didn't walk out of the house much. Our friends came to us, and those that didn't mind my new appearance became regular visitors."

Benny held Argyle's hand as her father was asked to show his demon aspect. The familiar features came and went.

Harcourt was dismissed, and Lenora was called to testify. She confirmed all of what had already been said.

"When I first held Benny in my arms, I was terrified of what the world would deliver to her. I wanted her safe, but I remembered how hard it was for me growing up. I wanted a better life for her and less power was the way to do it, at least at the time." Lenora sniffled. "It was all I could think of."

The gargoyle nodded and seemed at a loss for words. "Thank you, Missus Ganger. You may be seated."

The prosecutor looked befuddled, but the judge had a serious expression. "Court is in recess while I assess the testimony of those here today."

They all rose and left, the waiting room was quiet and Benny walked over to hug her parents. "I love you both."

Lenora stroked her cheek. "Thank you

for understanding, Benny."

Her dad gave her a firm bear hug. "You did well, Benny. It is better that we get things out in the open. Time to stop hiding."

"One way or another?"

"Precisely."

They waited for two hours until the chime rang again. When it pealed, they got up and walked back to the courtroom.

The judge sat, and he stared at everyone, slowly making eye contact with the defense and the prosecution. "This decision has not been an easy one. At this time, given the statute of limitations, there are no charges that would be relevant to the case at hand. While the families may pursue punitive damages, there are no criminal charges to be laid.

"Harcourt Emile Ganger is free to return to his home. His only crime is not investigating the actions of his wife when they were still at the hospital. Once the infants had left the building, there was nothing else to be done." The judge looked over those assembled.

"As the prosecution granted immunity to Lenora Ganger, there are no charges to pursue. If we were inclined to do so, the spell was cast on her own flesh and blood out of a post-partum protective instinct and therefore is not one that can legally be pursued. She has recovered, and her daughter was not materially harmed by the spell, the side effect has worn off with the death of the other women. All has reset to the point at which fate would have had it.

"I dismiss all culpability in this case on behalf of all the Gangers and wish them a more serene future. Case dismissed."

The prosecutor nodded, and his shoulders slumped with relief. The defense attorney smiled, and his wings opened as he stood. Her parents had paperwork to fill out, but they would be home before dawn.

Benny let the guys escort her out, and she braced herself for the court of public opinion. The courthouse steps were covered with folk waiting to see what was happening.

Jennifer was waiting with her family, and when Benny smiled at her, she rushed forward and hugged her. "I am so relieved."

"Your parents are free to sue mine if they choose to."

"I don't care. The tutor you set me up with is amazing." Jennifer mumbled it in Benny's ear.

"I am glad. He knows what he is talking about."

"We are looking into going into business together."

"Really?" Benny leaned back in surprise.

Jennifer grinned. "A coffee shop. We are thinking of naming it the Patchwork Dragon."

"I swear to be there on opening day."

"I will hold you to it. At this point, it is a few months away. It should be up and running just after winter holidays."

Benny was surprised. "Why so long?"

"I need to get my seer's license. A coffee shop run by a licensed seer would have had a certain cachet, and it means I can use my talent without going anywhere. All the magic will come to me."

"Good. If there is anything I can do, let me know."

"I will. Thanks for this new start. Good luck with your own." Jennifer winked and let her go.

Freddy came up and hugged her as they walked down to the sidewalk. The thud of hoof beats rang through the parking lot. They got on their steeds and took off for home. Folk may have been staring, but nothing was thrown. It was hard to hate the Wild Hunt. They were such beautiful horses.

A gallop through the wilds outside of town was just what she needed. When they got to the meadow, she was feeling soft satisfaction in the events of the night and far less panic.

News reports went over the bits of the case that were recorded and reported, as well as images of all of the Gangers were spread across the news and websites.

Benny spent time with her family, greeting old friends at the big house and introducing them to her new partners. Family came by, friends, acquaintances and a few curious folk who managed to work their way through the wards at the end of the street.

The new portions of their family also came by. The lions arrived and enjoyed a backyard barbeque as well as space to run around in whatever form they chose.

The vampires came with their own food and spent time socialising with the Gangers.

When the fey arrived, it was a party. Magic flared, enchantments spun and it was an experiment in who could make the most indecent-decent outfit. The combinations got peculiar.

As Tremble's sister pulled her aside, Benny knew what was coming.

"When are you going to have a wedding?"

"We are trying for the next full moon, but we might have to wait until we can find a way to make it legal. My parents are in full research mode."

She laughed, a light, lilting sound. "So, we are not the only eager parties?"

"Nope. Anyone who isn't in our party wants to know when we are getting married, and we have to wait for legal matters to catch up. We need a blood-bound dispensation, but for now, we are bonded and know it."

"True enough. Well, you are an interesting sister-in-law. I have never felt so much magic in such a small package."

Benny had come to grips with being short next to the other races. It was the most human thing about her.

"Does he really ride a member of the Wild Hunt?" His sister's tone was sly.

"Sure. Did you want to meet one?"

And so, the rest of Benny's night turned into arranging pony rides for elegant fey. It was not what she had expected, but it was something to kill time.

Arranging weddings with more than four distinct traditions was going to take some time. Lenora threw herself into it and into the new requests for both her and Harcourt to lecture at a number of nearby schools.

The lawsuits were also pending for using the babies as camouflage, but they could ask for what they wanted. If the families didn't have a history of financial success before the soul split, they would have to deduct all of the wages earned since their deceased daughters had begun working.

It was the same for the other young women. The pattern of success was a stain for those suing. Benny made money in a very specific way, and if her counterparts made money in the same method, their earnings belonged to her.

It was way too complicated.

Benny just wanted to get back to work, but they had to wait for the call. She hoped like hell that the call came soon.

Planning a wild wedding and defending a lawsuit at the same time was bizarre, and she desperately wanted a small sliver of normal back. *Pretty please.*

# Epilogue

The assembled XIA commanders and councillors kept their eyes fixed on the group.

In uniform, with her new badge highly polished, Benny stood with her partners and waited to find out what would happen next. Their little gathering had already had a number of job offers, consulting for a variety of species in regards to law enforcement and investigation, but they had all agreed that if they could, they would remain with the XIA.

The chairman of the meeting folded his hands in front of him. "Agents Smith, Tremble, Argyle and Ganger, this council has come to a decision regarding your continued employment by this agency."

Benny felt the tension fill her partners, and she mentally confessed to her own. They had not been asked for their opinion so—for once—Benny didn't offer it.

"While the circumstances of Agent Ganger's bloodline are unusual, they do provide us with an opportunity that the XIA has never had before."

Benny could feel Argyle perk up. His attention was well and fully captured. The other two were wary. She was willing to hear what was being offered.

"Since all charges against you and your family have been dropped as time served and there is still a bit of public unrest with your demon status, we have worked out an alternative."

A female councillor cleared her throat. "We are in need of a liaison to travel to cities and towns where new creatures are not being welcomed or are committing offenses. We need a gathering that can look human, go in and do what is necessary to secure the peace."

Benny blinked. "You want us...to look human?"

The councillor smiled. "We are aware that you can manage it and have managed it. The sharing of characteristics that you and your companions can engage in is on the record."

Benny wrinkled her nose. "Fair enough. May we discuss this for a moment?"

The council nodded and the woman said, "Of course."

Benny consulted her partners for a moment. They must have seemed strange to the watchers, but a heated debate raged across their joined thoughts. When they had a consensus, Argyle spoke.

"We agree to the arrangement on

principle, but we will need to see a document outlining our available courses of action. It will be held in confidence, but we wish to have the backing of this council when we act against the laws of a local area."

The serious folk looked at each other, and the councillor cleared her throat. "That is what we were attempting to tell you. While we will be able to offer you protection once you have entered the XIA territories, we are not welcome everywhere, and in those areas, you will have to protect yourselves. With that stipulation, will you consider this a new branch for investigations?"

Tremble eased forward. "When would we commence our new branch of investigations?"

The captain leaned down and heaved up a box of files. "Each of these files contains a person or persons in a settlement who is hiding who they are from a town or family that would persecute or destroy them. The extra-naturals need to be removed, rescued or arrested, and the locals are not able to manage it. If you accept this arrangement, you begin immediately."

After another silent consultation, Benny smiled, "Show us the contract and let's get this started."

One by one, they signed a contract that was hiring them as investigative consultants under the banner of the XIA. There were new extra-naturals coming into power that needed their help, and there was nothing like a well-balanced team to help out when it was needed. It would get them out, let them travel and give the steeds a chance to run.

Benny put her signature and a spot of blood beneath that of her partners. She was doing it for the steeds, really.

After all, Benny had all the opportunities to exert herself that she could want.

Whew! Well, I did it. I planned for the first three books in the Obscure Magic series and they were done.

Personally, I had a problem during this book. My father passed away suddenly, halfway through. I tried my best to keep it going, but my heart wasn't in it.

An Obscure Magic returns Jan. 1, 2016. We will delve into the lives of some of the ladies we have met on the way...and Benny and the boys will pop up when you least expect them.

*Ritual Space, Hell in a Handbag, Defying Eternity, Chosen and Slain,* are a few of the titles lying in wait.

In the meantime, there is a holiday series of nine books beginning on Oct 26 and culminating on Dec. 24. The first book is titled *Dear Santa, Get Bent.* When the reindeer have had enough of enforced celibacy, they break out and make a run for the human world in an effort to...socialise. The elves of the Naughty and Nice list are sent out in *Operation Reindeer Retrieval,* to bring the ladies home by whatever means necessary.

Thanks for reading,

Viola Grace

*www.violagrace.com*
*http://www.violagrace.com*

# About the Author

Viola Grace (aka Zenina Masters) is a Canadian sci-fi/paranormal romance writer with ambitions to keep writing for the rest of her life. She specialises in short stories because the thrill of discovery, of all those firsts, is what keeps her writing.

An artist who enjoys a story that catches you up, whirls you around and sets you down with a smile on your face is all she endeavours to be. She prefers to leave the drama to those who are better suited to it; she always goes for the cheap laugh.